MAIL ORDER MADNESS

BRIDES OF BECKHAM BOOK THREE

KIRSTEN OSBOURNE

UNLIMITED DREAMS

Susan cannot stand living with her eleven younger siblings for another minute, so she answers an advertisement for a mail order bride, carefully choosing a man who has never married and has no children so she won't be plagued with other people's ill-behaved offspring. When she arrives in Fort Worth, she finds out her fiancé has been killed, and his older brother is offering to take his place. The only problem is his brother is a widower with four young boys. Dare she do it?

CHAPTER 1

*J*une 1884
Outside of Beckham, Massachusetts

SUSAN BREATHED a sigh of relief as her day with the neighbor children was finally over. It wasn't that the Jacobs' kids were bad, because her own siblings made them look like angels, but she was just tired of being around children all the time. Everywhere she looked were kids getting into everything. She thought, not for the first time, that she needed to get married and escape everyone else's children. She knew without a doubt, that she could make sure her own kids, if God cursed her with them, behaved well.

She wandered along the dirt road, breathing deeply of the warm summer air. There were flowers in bloom all around her and the trees overhead made a perfect covering protecting her from the hot sun. Summer was her favorite season of the year. She wondered if she'd have time to go for a quick dip in the family's pond after dinner.

She walked the quarter of a mile to her family's farm and went inside, knowing it was time for her to help with dinner. Her sister who was two years younger than her at sixteen had been home with their younger siblings all day, and since there were ten younger siblings, she knew the job would be overwhelming for her sister.

Their mother worked in town for one of the women there cleaning and doing odd jobs around the house. Ever since her youngest brother had broken his arm the previous month, her mother had needed to work to help make ends meet. Their small dairy farm just wasn't enough to support all fourteen of them and pay any doctor bills that came along.

Susan walked through the kitchen and noted the absence of anything cooking. There were egg shells and smashed egg yolks all over the walls and floor. Where was Elizabeth?

She found her in the small parlor with her head in her hands crying. Sitting beside Elizabeth on the sofa, Susan asked, "What'd they do now?"

Elizabeth rubbed her eyes. She was small for her age, and not much bigger than some of their younger brothers. She had the same blond hair and green eyes Susan did, but at that moment, her eyes were red-rimmed and her hair was sticking up in every direction. Susan thought she detected a piece of egg shell in her sister's hair, but didn't say anything about it. "I cannot do this anymore! They're hellions!" She threw her hands up in the air in defeat.

"Egg fight?" Susan knew there'd been a pretty major egg fight in the kitchen, but that was nothing new in their house. Why would Elizabeth be so upset over something like that?

Elizabeth nodded. "To start with." She took a deep breath. "Have you seen the outhouse? Or been in the barn yet?"

"No...." What had the monsters done this time?

"Well, first they had the egg fight in the kitchen. I walked in and yelled for them to stop before one of the twins beaned me in the side of the head with an egg. I was about to clean it up, but I had to answer nature's call first." Susan nodded, waiting for her sister to get to what the kids had done. "They tipped over the outhouse…with me in it!"

Susan pressed her hand to her mouth to hide the grin that wanted to pop out. It wasn't funny, and she'd be furious if it had been her, but she couldn't help the laughter that was trying to bubble up and out of her. In retrospect the things their siblings did were funny, but it took a while to find enough distance to laugh when you'd been the victim of their mischief.

"Then, when I finally got out and was coming back in the house, I saw Mary's hands were covered with paint. Lavender paint. You know the paint Ma said we could use to paint our room?" Mary was their ten year old sister. She was the next-oldest girl after Elizabeth and the three of them shared a room.

"Yes?"

"Well, she didn't want a purple room, so she used the paint on Mabel."

"Mabel? She actually stood still for that?"

"She wasn't happy. I could hear her mooing from across the yard. Apparently, Mary pulled her in from the field where she was grazing and put her in her stall, before painting her lavender." Elizabeth sighed. "So no pretty room for us. We have to put up with the tic tac toe game on the walls forever."

Susan sighed heavily. "I've got to get out of here. I'm eighteen. I should be married by now and I wouldn't have to put up with this nonsense anymore." She stared off into space for a moment while she thought about it. "Or I guess I could find a job where I could live in. But no kids!"

Elizabeth shook her head. "Then I'd have to deal with them all without you. Ma doesn't much care what they do,

3

and I can't do it alone." Susan's eyes looked fearful at the very idea of Susan leaving her there with the monsters.

"I hate to leave you in this situation by yourself, but honestly? I'm doing it the first chance I get." She looked around. "What happened to the newspaper Pa brought home yesterday?"

"Mary had Mabel stand on it so she wouldn't get paint on the floor of the barn."

That was finally too much for Susan and she felt the laugh rumble up from inside her. "So it's okay to paint the cow, but not to paint the barn floor? Did she get dropped on her *head* when she was a baby?"

"It's not funny! You don't have to stay here with them all day every day. At least you get to go to the Jacobs' farm three days a week. I want to go to the Jacob's farm." Elizabeth's voice was usually calm and serene, but it had deteriorated to a whine.

"We should walk into town together after supper and get a newspaper. Maybe we can find you a job, too." Susan had made up her mind during her conversation with her sister. She was going to get out no matter what she had to do.

"Okay. But what are we going to fix for supper? It'll be time to eat in an hour."

Susan stood up and held her hand out for her sister. "We'll figure something out. And then we'll figure out how to get out of here!"

As they walked into town two hours later, the two sisters talked about their dreams for the future. "I want to be a teacher," Elizabeth admitted. "I don't think I ever want to get married."

Susan grinned. "Just so you don't have to teach our brothers and sisters!" Not getting married was a good idea, in a way, because then she would never be saddled with children, but Susan wanted to find a man to love her.

Elizabeth finally saw the humor in her day and giggled a little. "I want to be a teacher in Oregon. Or California. I hear California is beautiful this time of year." She stopped walking and looked at Susan with fear in her eyes. "You don't think Ma and Pa would ever move to California, do you?"

Susan shook her head, pulling her sister along with her. "That's a better plan." She kicked at a clump of dirt along her path as she walked. They were almost to Beckham. "I really wish I could just get married, but where am I going to meet a man? We go to the same country church we've gone to our whole lives, and the most eligible bachelor is old James Duncan."

Elizabeth wrinkled her nose. "He does seem interested in you." James Duncan was seventy if he was a day, and he'd already buried four wives. He was on the prowl for number five, and Susan seemed to be the object of his affections.

Susan let out a shudder. "I don't think so." They'd reached town and turned to the general store, which was closed, but always set out the "old" newspapers at the end of the day.

Each sister took one, and they settled themselves onto the bench in front of the store to scan the job advertisements. Susan quickly scanned through and stopped at an advertisement for mail order brides. "Mail Order Bride agency needs women who are looking for the adventure of their lives. Men out West need women to marry. Reply in person at 300 Rock Creek Road. See Mrs. Harriett Long."

Elizabeth looked at Susan. "Nothing for me, but did you see the ad for a Mail Order Bride?"

Susan nodded slowly. "I just read it. Am I really desperate enough to get away to answer it, though?" She bit her lip thinking hard about whether that was something she really wanted to do.

"I am! If I wanted to get married and get away from 'the

demon horde' we call brothers and sisters I would do it in a heartbeat."

Susan made up her mind to do it. What could it hurt to just talk to the woman? "Would you go to see Mrs. Long with me?"

Elizabeth looked back down at the paper. "Rock Creek Road. Do you know where that is?"

"I think it's in the rich part of town." Susan's brows drew together. "Why would a rich woman run a mail order bride business?"

"I have no idea." She stood and held her hand out for her sister. "Let's go see if we can find Rock Creek Road."

"You mean it?" Susan had expected Elizabeth to try to talk her out of going, but instead she supported her. She was a good sister.

Elizabeth nodded. "One of us should be able to get out of there!"

Susan took Elizabeth's hand and the two of them walked toward the rich side of town, stopping once to get directions. Once they were in front of the house on Rock Creek Road, Susan's eyes grew wide and she looked at her sister. "This place is huge."

Elizabeth was obviously awestruck. "And beautiful." The two girls stared at the house in awe for a minute.

"How's my hair?" Susan asked.

Elizabeth sighed. "As good as it ever is." They both knew Susan's long blond hair hated to be confined in a bun. There were always tendrils popping out of any hairdo she tried to put it in. There was nothing to do about it now, though. "Let's go up."

"Are you coming in with me?"

"If you want me to."

"Oh, I do! I don't think I could knock on that door without you beside me." Susan wasn't shy, but there was something about the mansion in front of them that intimidated her. She didn't really want to take her sister, but she didn't feel like she could do it alone.

"Let's go then."

The two sisters walked slowly up the sidewalk to the front door. Susan reached out and knocked three times, holding her breath as she waited for someone to come to the door.

It was answered within moments by a tall thin man with dark hair and eyes. "May I help you?"

Susan stared at him for a moment. He seemed to fit in well with the home and she couldn't help but wonder if the owners had bought him as part of it. Elizabeth elbowed her in the side to get her to talk. "I'm here to see Mrs. Long, please."

The man seemed to take them in all at once. His eyes dropped to the newspapers in their hands and he gave a quick nod. "Of course. Mrs. Long is in her office. If you'd come this way?" He led the way toward the back of a long elegant hallway.

Susan wanted to pop her head into every room and see what was behind the closed doors. She'd seen houses like this before, but she'd never been inside one, and she found she wanted to know everything about it.

The man stopped at a door at the end of the hallway, and knocked once, before opening the door. "There are two young ladies here to see you, ma'am."

Susan couldn't see inside the room, but a soft musical voice responded. "Thank you, Higgins. Would you bring some refreshments for us please?"

"Yes, of course." He held the door wide while the two girls found their way in and closed it softly behind them.

Susan looked around the small room they were in. There was a desk with an office chair and a sofa as well as an overstuffed comfortable chair. She felt they were horribly under-dressed and wished she had thought to go home and change before they had gone there. She was still wearing the dirty dress she'd watched the children in, and although she'd put her shoes and socks on before leaving the house, she knew her feet were filthy from going barefoot all day even if the pretty lady before her didn't.

Mrs. Long slowly got to her feet and limped the few steps toward the girls. "I'm Harriett Long." When Susan and Elizabeth just stared at her, she smiled and held her hand out. "And you are?"

Susan cleared her throat with embarrassment. "I'm Susan Miller, and this is my sister, Elizabeth. We've come about your advertisement for mail order brides."

Harriett looked between the two sisters. "Have a seat. Are both of you interested in becoming brides?"

Susan shook her head. "No, just me. Elizabeth is just here for moral support." Susan squeezed her sister's hand in silent thanks for going with her.

Harriett smiled as the girls finally sat down on the sofa and she returned to her seat in front of the desk. "Why don't you tell me a little about yourself then, Susan? What makes you interested in becoming a mail order bride?"

"Honestly, it's our home situation."

Harriett's brows drew together quickly. "Are you mistreated by your parents?"

Susan let out a slight laugh. "Oh, no. It's not that at all. In fact, our parents need to find a switch and start using it. Often." She paused for a moment looking at Elizabeth who was grinning at her. "I'm the oldest of twelve children. The oldest four, Elizabeth and I and our two oldest brothers, Michael and Henry, were all strongly disciplined from the beginning. We were raised to take responsibility for our actions. After the four of us, mother just got tired, I think."

"How so?" Harriett's eyes were on Susan's and she was taking in every word the younger woman said. It was as if Susan were imparting important knowledge.

"Well, our younger siblings are…." She didn't want to use the word hellions, but that and "demon horde" were the only words that came to mind. She bit her lip for a moment.

"Satan's spawn." The words, loud and clear and unashamed, came from Elizabeth.

Harriett choked back a laugh. "That bad?" She picked up the cup of tea Higgins had brought to them and took a sip.

Susan nodded emphatically. "Worse. Anyway, I've got to get out of there. My one stipulation for a husband is he must not have any children. If God curses me with children of my own, I'll raise them with a strict hand and a long switch." She needed to get that out of the way to begin with. She was not going to raise some man's problems.

Harriett smiled, obviously delighted by the honesty of the young women sitting in front of her. "How old are you, Susan? I won't send out a woman younger than eighteen."

"I was eighteen in March."

"Well, let's see then." Harriett turned to her desk and flipped through the different letters there. "No, he has children," she mumbled. She finally found a letter halfway through her stack and read through it quickly. "He's the one I was looking for. I think Jesse Dailey is just the man you're looking for." She handed the letter to Susan for her to read.

Susan opened the letter and held it to where Elizabeth could read it along with her. It struck her that as much as she wanted to get away from 'the demon horde' she would miss Elizabeth just as much. Elizabeth had always been more than a sister. She was her best friend. She made a silent vow to tell her so before she left.

"Dear potential bride, My name is Jesse Dailey and I'm a newspaperman in Fort Worth, Texas. I hope to be able to buy a ranch in the area soon, so I'm looking for a bride who is willing to save every penny to help me toward that goal. I'm not sure what to tell you about myself, so I'm just going to ramble for a bit. I'm tall with dark hair and brown eyes. I've lived in Texas my entire life, and grew up on a ranch here. I enjoy quiet walks in the country and reading. I go to church every Sunday. I'm well-respected in town as a hard-hitting newspaperman who makes sure he always tells the truth, even if it's not what people want to hear. I'm twenty-three years old and have never married. I enjoy a good home cooked meal, and would request my bride be able to cook. I'd like someone between the ages of eighteen and twenty-two. I'm looking forward to getting married and settling down. All the best, Jesse."

Susan smiled as she read he wanted someone who could cook. She'd been cooking for years and knew there would be no trouble there. She certainly matched his requests. She looked up at Harriett. "I'll take him."

Harriett laughed. "He's not just a man on the shelf that you can choose. You need to write him back and we'll go from there." She handed Susan a pen, ink and paper. "Go ahead and write the letter now. All correspondence needs to go through me."

Susan took the pen and dipped it into the ink well. What to write? After a moment of thinking, she put the pen to paper. "Dear Jesse, My name is Susan Miller. I live on a small farm outside of Beckham, Massachusetts with my parents and my eleven younger brothers and sisters. I'm eighteen years old and I'm a good cook. I'd love to cook for just two people instead of fourteen. I also enjoy long walks through the country and reading books, although I rarely have free time to do either one. I do not mind living frugally, because it's the only way I know. I am of medium height and have blond hair and green eyes. I've never been to Texas, but I've read about it some, and find it fascinating. I'd love to move there to be your bride." Susan set the pen down and read the letter aloud, making sure Mrs. Long approved of what she'd written.

Harriett nodded. "That's perfect. Sign it, and I'll send it off with the morning's mail."

Susan quickly signed her name to the bottom and handed the unfolded paper to the older woman. "Now what?"

"Come see me in about a month to see what he says. If he decides you're the one he wants, he'll send you some money for the trip to Texas, and a train ticket."

"Sounds good." Susan stood up, realizing she hadn't touched the tea and cookies Higgins had brought in while she was working on her letter. She grabbed a cookie from the plate. "Thank you so much." She held her hand out to Mrs. Long. "I'll see you in about a month, I guess."

Harriett got to her feet slowly. "I look forward to it." She smiled at Elizabeth. "It was nice meeting you, Elizabeth." She walked the two sisters to the front door and watched them walk away, smiling to herself.

ONE MONTH LATER, Susan knocked on Harriett's door. She'd had to sneak away from the farm to come into town, because her younger siblings would have begged to come with her. She could just imagine the mischief they would get into in a house like Mrs. Long's. *There would be nothing left but rubble,* she thought.

Higgins answered the door promptly. "Come right in." He opened the door wide and led her to the office again. He knocked once and opened the office door. "Miss Miller is here to see you, Ma'am. I'll get some refreshments." He closed the door softly behind him.

Harriett got to her feet and smiled as Susan walked in. Susan couldn't help but wonder what had happened to the older woman to make her move so slowly. She obviously had an injured leg, but how had it been injured? She'd been taught not to ask such things, but she certainly wanted to.

Harriett waved to the sofa. "Have a seat. Your letter came just this morning, so this is good timing." Once Susan was seated, Harriett handed her the letter. "I didn't open it, because it's addressed to you." She turned away to look through some papers on her desk and to give Susan a bit of privacy with her letter.

Susan took a deep breath before opening the letter. She desperately wanted there to be a train ticket inside. As soon as she opened it, a train ticket, a check and some cash fell out. She smiled, knowing he wanted her. She picked up the check, which was made out to Mrs. Harriett Long, and handed it to her. She picked up the cash and showed Harriett. "Is this for me to keep?"

Harriett nodded. "It's for any expenses you may have. Your train ride will be a long one, so you'll want to keep at least half of that for food on the train. The rest you can use for clothes or anything else you may need." She paused for a moment. "What's the date on the ticket?"

Susan looked down to check. "I leave July twenty eighth. That's a Monday, right?"

Harriett checked her calendar. "It is. That gives you ten days. Do you think you can get clothes made in time?"

Susan thought about it. "If Elizabeth and I ignore all the kids, we can probably get a couple of dresses made. Do I need a formal wedding dress?"

"I usually say 'yes' to that. See if he mentioned the wedding in his letter." Harriett indicated the letter in the younger woman's hand.

Susan looked down and laughed at herself. She'd been so

excited about the train ticket she hadn't bothered to read the letter. "I guess I should read it, shouldn't I?"

Harriett grinned. "I know you're excited to get away, so I won't say anything."

"Dear Susan, I'm so excited you answered my letter. You sound like you're going to fill the missing space in my life perfectly. I've enclosed a train ticket for Monday, July twenty eighth. I will be waiting for you at the train station in Fort Worth on Wednesday, August sixth. I'll carry a sign with your name on it, so you'll know immediately who I am. I'm not going to subject you to a big wedding after your long trip, so I will arrange for us to marry at the courthouse with just my brother and his children present. I hope that meets with your approval. If it's a problem, you can let me know when you get here, and we'll make other arrangements. I can't wait to meet you. Yours, Jesse."

"He said we'd just marry at the courthouse. I think I'll just make a new Sunday dress. That's better than spending a lot of money on a gown I'll only wear one time."

Harriett nodded. "May I read the letter?"

Susan didn't feel any real attachment for Jesse, and he hadn't put anything private in the letter, so she readily agreed, handing it to Harriett.

Susan studied the older woman while her head was bowed reading the letter. If you ignored their dress, Harriett could have been her sister. She looked to be around twenty-eight and had blond hair and green eyes. She was slim and seemed very graceful despite her pronounced limp.

"Everything looks good here. The train ride is a long one. You're not going to have a chance to bathe or anything once you're on the train. That's one of the biggest complaints of my brides. Will that bother you?"

Susan made a face. She didn't like the idea of going for over a week without a bath, but it would be worth it to get married and away from her family once and for all. "I'll manage."

"Most men do make some kind of arrangement for you to bathe before your wedding, I've found."

"Good. I can't imagine getting married without at least bathing first." The idea of a long train ride was both exciting and daunting.

"I can't imagine that either." Harriett studied the younger woman for a moment. "Would you like me to see you off? I do that for most of the brides I send out."

Susan thought about that for a few seconds. "I think that would be good. I'm sure Elizabeth will be there if she can, but I have no way of knowing whether she'll be able to get away or not."

"What time does your train leave on Wednesday?"

"Eight in the morning."

"Come by here at seven and we'll walk to the train station together. We can talk on the way. If your sister comes, great. Then there will be two of us to see you off."

Harriett stood and led Susan to the door. On impulse, Susan turned and hugged Harriett before leaving. "Thank you so much. You've helped me a lot."

"It's my job to help as much as I can. I think of each of my brides as a friend."

Susan thought about Harriett's words as she walked to the general store just a few streets over. Beckham wasn't a large city, so nothing was very far apart.

Once she got to the store, she went inside, looking at fabrics for some new dresses. Everything she owned had once belonged to her mother and had been cut down for her. Jesse had been generous with the money he'd sent, and although she knew she needed some for the trip, she could buy enough fabric for three or four dresses without a problem.

She flipped through the bolts of cloth and picked out a pink with small flowers, a blue check, a pretty lavender, which she realized matched the cow exactly, and a forest green to match her eyes. She also bought an entire bolt of white linen for new undergarments. She couldn't wait to get home to start sewing.

After paying for her purchases, she carried the small wooden box the shopkeeper had given her home. Her mind was full of how perfect life would be without poorly behaved children climbing all over her. Oh, she had no illusions. She knew someday she'd have children too. Her mother had twelve for goodness sakes! But she would have some time before the children arrived to just be Susan. She loved the idea of just taking care of laundry and cooking and cleaning for two people. She sighed. Life would be heavenly.

≈

JULY 1884

Outside of Fort Worth, Texas

JESSE DAILEY TOOK a gulp of his water as he watched his four young nephews run around his brother's house screaming. The four of them had been causing his brother problems ever since his sister-in-law, Caroline, had died at the birth of two year old twins, Thomas and Walter. He shook his head at his brother wondering just how he could live amidst the chaos. "I have news."

David raised his eyebrow waiting. "You found a ranch?"

Jesse shook his head. "Not yet, but I'm saving every penny." He folded his hands behind his head and leaned back in the kitchen chair. He'd just had a good meal, thanks to his brother's cook and housekeeper, Sadie. "I'm getting married."

David's jaw dropped. "Married! I didn't even know you were courting anyone."

Jesse grinned. "I don't have time to court anyone. Not with spending every waking moment at the newspaper office, picking up extra articles so I can make enough to buy a ranch. I like being a reporter, but my heart is in ranching. I should have been the big brother."

David laughed. "I've told you a hundred times, you're welcome to half the ranch. You can even live here with the boys and me while you build yourself a house." He kicked his brother's foot affectionately. "Who's the girl?" He reached for a cookie and popped half of it into his mouth.

"I sent for a mail order bride." Jesse said the words nonchalantly, knowing they'd surprise his brother.

David choked on his cookie. After a moment, his eyes watering, he asked, "Seriously?"

"Seriously. She's going to be here in a couple of weeks. You coming to the wedding? I'm just going to do a courthouse thing. No need for a big church wedding when she doesn't know anyone here."

"Of course, I'll be there. Girl got a name?" David studied his younger brother as if he was trying to decide if he'd lost his mind.

Jesse's brow furrowed. "Susan." He thought over the details of her letter. "She's 18 and the oldest of twelve kids. Says she can cook. I think she's just ready to get out of Massachusetts."

David nodded. "I'll watch and see how it works out for you, and I may do the same." He jerked his thumb over his shoulder to where his older two boys were pointing imaginary guns at each other and screaming and his two youngest were pushing each other. "I'll never get a bride who knows me and my brood. I need one who is unsuspecting."

Jesse laughed and clapped his brother on the shoulder. "You have a point."

David sighed. "Sure would be nice to have a warm body in bed at night again, though. A man gets lonely."

"I thought you were going to court that sweet nanny of yours." He looked around, realizing she wasn't there. "Where is she anyway?"

"Where do you think? After the boys put a toad in her bed for the third time this week, she left. She said, 'I'm not going to stay here another minute with your boys. They're monsters.' Then she stuck a finger in my face and told me if I didn't find a good woman to be their mother and take them in hand, they'd be ruined forever." He shrugged. "I guess she wasn't volunteering to be that good woman."

Jesse shook his head, sympathizing. David had dealt with the four boys on his own for a year, before deciding to find himself a wife. He hadn't felt right about remarrying before that. By that time the boys had been running wild for too long, and their behavior showed it. "Maybe a mail order bride is something you need to do. Next time I see you, I'll give you the address of the woman in Massachusetts that runs the agency I used." He stood up. "I've got to go. I promised my editor I'd run to Hell's Half Acre tonight to do a story on a man who was murdered there."

David made a face. "Be careful. The Acre gets worse every year. Do you have anyone who can go with you?"

Jesse shrugged. "I was going to ask you, but you seem to be without a nanny for the boys." Again.

"Yeah, I'd go, but it's not a good time. Find someone, though. You really shouldn't go there alone. Especially at night." He looked out the window. It was dusk, but by the time Jesse made it back to town it would be full night. "Be really careful whether someone's with you or not." He made a face. "Maybe you should wait until daylight."

"I'll be okay, big brother. I've been taking care of myself for several years now."

David stood up and hugged his brother. "Take care."

Jesse yelled over the din, "Goodbye monster children! I'll be back!"

Albert and Lewis looked up from their game of cowboys and Indians and ran over to hug their uncle. "See you at church!"

The two younger boys ignored him as usual. With a last wave, he left, riding into town to find out what had happened to Joshua Campbell, a man who had died there the previous evening. He didn't have time to find someone to go with him, so he went alone. He'd be okay. He'd been in The Acre for stories lots of times. Just never at night.

CHAPTER 2

*S*usan made the two mile walk home carrying her box of fabric. She wanted to start sewing immediately, but knew she still had to do her three day per week job for the Jacobs. She wondered if Elizabeth could take over there. Of course, that would leave Mary in charge of the younger siblings, and Mary was only ten. Whatever happened, they'd make it work.

When Susan arrived at home, she saw her mother was already there. Ma usually worked until at least six, so Susan was surprised to see her before five. Susan walked up behind her in the kitchen and kissed her cheek, before asking, "What are you doing home already?"

Lucy Miller turned and smiled at her eldest child. "We finally got enough money saved up to pay off the doctor bills. I'm home for good again." She turned back to the stew she was making, carefully dropping in the potatoes and carrots she'd peeled and chunked. "What have you been off buying?"

Susan sighed. She probably should have talked to her parents about her plans already, but they were always so busy she hated to bother them with little things. Of course, her moving to Texas to marry wasn't exactly a little thing. "We need to talk for a minute, Ma."

Lucy turned back to Susan when she heard the serious tone to her voice. "What's wrong?"

Susan put the box down on the kitchen table. "Nothing's *wrong*. I'm getting married and moving to Fort Worth, Texas." She said the words quickly to get them over with.

Lucy put down the spoon she was using to stir the stew and sat down at the table. "Sit and tell me everything." Her face remained calm as she waited for her daughter to explain what was going on.

Susan sat down in the chair next to her mother and turned to her fully. She quickly explained about the mail order bride service.

"Why do you want to be married so badly you're not willing to wait for nature to take its course? I'm sure you'll find a young man here."

Susan sighed. "Honestly? There's no one in our whole church except old man Duncan, and I'm not marrying him. I just want to get away and start my own life." She paused. "And the kids are out of control. It's hard to live here, Ma." She felt bad being the one to break the news to her mother, but someone needed to tell her how bad things had gotten.

Lucy nodded. "I'm going to whip the kids into shape now that I'm not working."

Susan almost laughed. The kids had been out of control for years. Her mother just wasn't willing to be as strict with the younger ones as she'd been with her four oldest. Susan didn't believe she'd do a thing to get the kids behaving better. Well, to her credit, she'd probably work hard at it for a day or two, and then she'd give up when she remembered how hard it was. "My train leaves in ten days, Ma."

"Train? You already have a ticket?" Lucy looked hurt that

Susan had made as many plans as she had without consulting her first.

Susan nodded. "Look. I bought all of this fabric so we can make me some pretty clothes to start my married life with. Would you help me? Elizabeth already said she'd take over my job at the Jacobs' house."

Lucy bit her lip, obviously fighting tears. "Of course, I'll help you. You'll have the prettiest clothes any new bride ever had." She stood up and dug through the box Susan had brought home. "Which do you want your Sunday dress made from?" She held up the different fabrics to Susan's face to see which she thought suited her best. "I can't quite decide between the pink and the green. What do you think?"

Susan wanted to jump up and hug her mother to thank her for agreeing and helping so quickly. She knew her ma didn't want her to go, but she was helping anyway. "Umm…I think I like the green for my Sunday dress if you think that's okay. I'll be getting married in my Sunday dress as well. Is green okay to get married in?"

Lucy nodded. "The green is perfect." She took the fabric and laid it out on the table. "Go get my sewing shears. We're going to have this cut out before everyone comes in for dinner."

They worked together quickly, knowing their time before the family came in was limited. Susan filled the silence by telling her mother everything she knew about Jesse. "I promise I'll write as soon as I get there."

Elizabeth came in an hour before dinner, having taken on a babysitting job for one of the neighbors for the afternoon. When she saw what Susan and her mother were doing, she smiled. "I'm not sure if I should be happy for my sister or sad for myself."

Susan turned to her sister, and best friend, and hugged

her. "Just be happy for me. I'll write so often, you'll be sick of my letters."

Elizabeth smiled through her tears. "You'd better." She walked to the table and looked at their mother. "I guess you know everything and are willing to help."

Lucy shrugged. "Susan's an adult. It doesn't much matter if I agree or not. I'm going to help my daughter, though." She made the last cut and moved the scraps together. "I think we can make you a nice bonnet to match out of the leftover fabric."

"That will be wonderful. I don't know much about Texas, but I do know it's supposed to be hot. A bonnet will be necessary to keep the sun off my face." Susan helped her mother gather up the pieces they'd cut.

Lucy quickly spread out the scraps and cut the first piece for a bonnet. "This will be perfect for wearing to church." She suddenly looked up, startled. "He does go to church doesn't he?"

Susan exchanged a look with Elizabeth. "Yes, Ma. He said in his letter that he goes to church every Sunday." She knew it was important to her mother that she marry a Christian, and it was important to her as well.

Lucy sighed, looking relieved. "Well at least you're not traveling to the middle of nowhere to marry a heathen."

Susan and Elizabeth both giggled. "I wouldn't have agreed to marry him if he'd been a heathen."

Lucy shrugged. "You never can tell. Marrying a man you've never met, heathen or not, is daring enough." She finished the last cut on the bonnet. "Your father isn't going to be happy, you know."

"Pa will understand. And that's one less mouth to feed," Susan pointed out realistically.

"Our children are not a burden," Lucy said with a serious

look. "You don't think you're a burden, do you? Is that why you're doing this?"

"No, of course not! I just think it's time for me to have my own life. I'm finished with school, and I just watch the neighbor kids and help with my brothers and sisters all day. It's time for me to start my own life. It was either marry or find a full time job somewhere."

Lucy nodded. "I do think you'll do well in marriage. I just hate the idea of you moving so far away. What if he's not a good man?"

"Then I'll come back home. I'm not afraid to admit when I've made a mistake." Susan meant it too. She was strong enough and confident enough that if she found herself married to a bad man, she'd leave so fast he wouldn't know what happened.

The words seemed to relieve Lucy's fears. The three women worked together to get the sewing off the table, so they could set it for dinner.

The family straggled in over the next few minutes to wash their hands and sit down at the kitchen table for their meal. They all joined hands as their father, Norman, said a prayer over the meal. "Thank you, Lord, for the meal we're about to eat. Amen."

As soon as Norman picked up his spoon to eat his first bite of stew, Lucy said, "Norman, Susan has some big news to share."

Norman looked at his eldest daughter, cautiously spooning a bite of stew into his mouth. The different cooks in the house made things very differently. Young Mary would attempt meals that had to be fed to the hogs. His lined face showed he appreciated the fact the meal was cooked by someone who know what she was doing. "What's your news, Susan?"

Susan hadn't expected her mother to immediately put her

on the spot and used her spoon to stir her stew for a second before meeting her father's eyes. He was so much harder to talk to than her mother. "I'm getting married and moving to Texas, Pa." She kept her voice steady and her eyes on her father's as she said the words.

Norman looked bewildered for a moment and all talking stopped at the table. Susan's younger siblings stared at her in shock. After a moment, Norman said, "Who are you marrying?"

"His name is Jesse Dailey. He's a newspaperman in Fort Worth." Susan waited for the negative reaction, but it never came.

"When will you leave?" Norman looked resigned to the fact he'd lost his oldest daughter.

"In ten days."

He nodded slowly. "We'll have to get you a nice new carpet bag to take with you."

"I'd really appreciate that, Pa." Her eyes told him she appreciated his support.

Norman met Lucy's eyes. "Are you helping her make new clothes? She can't go out there to be a bride with the old clothes she has."

Lucy nodded, her eyes shining. "We cut out her Sunday dress before supper. I'll have Susan, Elizabeth, and Mary sew on the dress as soon as the dishes are done, and I'll cut out the next dress. I'd like to get four dresses, bonnets, and underwear made before she goes. And a couple of new aprons, too. She'll need aprons if she's going to be a wife."

Norman looked at his two oldest boys, both of whom were exhausted from helping him in the fields all day. "Michael, Henry, we're going to be watching the children in the evenings until the sewing is done." When Michael, who was the oldest brother at fifteen, started to protest, Norman held up a hand. "Your sister has made a lot of meals for you and made your beds more times than I can count. You'll do this to help her out."

Both of the boys nodded reluctantly.

Once dinner was over, everyone sprang into action. Elizabeth and Mary took care of the dinner dishes, while Susan started stitching her Sunday dress. Lucy quickly cut out into the fabric. Her daughter wasn't going to Texas looking like a pauper.

That night set a pattern for the days to come. Every day, Susan, Lucy and Mary sewed until their fingers ached while Elizabeth helped when she could around taking care of the Jacobs' children.

Sunday night, Susan and Lucy stayed up until the wee hours finishing up Susan's underwear and nightgowns. It was after two in the morning when Susan snipped the thread from her last nightgown. It was a plain white gown that went all the way to her feet, but there were ruffles on the bodice to make it prettier. Lucy had convinced Susan to make the nightgowns short sleeved, because the summer weather in Texas would be stifling.

Susan held it up in front of her to show Lucy. "What do you think, Ma?"

Lucy nodded, blinking her eyes to try to stay awake as she finished the last of the underwear. "Looks good."

Susan folded it and placed it into the mostly filled new carpet bag her parents had bought her as a wedding gift. She then went to the mantle and took the money that was left from her purchases and put it into a small string purse she'd purchased. "Do you think I have everything I need?"

Lucy thought for a moment. "I think we've covered everything. In the morning, we'll pack several sandwiches for your first day on the train to save you a little money, but after that, you'll be paying for your meals. I've heard a small box of candy on a train can cost as much as ten cents! Of course, I've never been on a train, so that could be an exaggeration."

Susan hadn't considered the idea she was doing something her mother had never done by taking the train. "Have you been to Texas?"

Lucy laughed. "I've never been out of Massachusetts. Texas sounds like a far-away land to me."

"Maybe you and Pa could come visit me in Fort Worth sometime." She had known she was going to miss Elizabeth, but hadn't really thought about missing her parents. The hours and hours of constant sewing she'd spent in the past week and a half had reminded her how much she would miss her mother.

"Maybe someday."

Susan knew Lucy could make no promises, because she would have children at home for at least another sixteen years. "I hope we can see each other again someday."

"So do I." Lucy bit off the thread and handed the last undergarment to Susan. "We both need to get to bed. I'll take you into town in the wagon in the morning."

Susan bit her lip, hating the idea of asking her mother to do more for her than she already had. "You don't have to, Ma. It's only a two mile walk to Mrs. Long's house. She's going to see me off."

"I'll drop you at her house then. I've let things slack around here the last couple of weeks, so I'll come straight back."

"Thanks, Ma." Even though it was unnecessary, Susan appreciated her mother's insistence on driving her to Harriett's house. It made her feel like her decision to move away was supported completely by her parents.

Susan packed the last of her things into the bag and closed it. She was amazed. "I thought this was too big when

Pa brought it home, but it's completely full. I had no idea I had so many things!"

Lucy smiled. "You didn't two weeks ago." She eyed the carpet bag. "I think you'll have plenty to start your marriage."

"Thanks for all your help, Ma. I know you have reservations about me marrying this way, and I appreciate you getting past them to work so hard to help me."

"You're my oldest daughter. I'm going to give you the best send-off I can. I hope your marriage is everything you want it to be." Lucy pulled Susan into her arms and held her close for a minute. "It seems like just yesterday I was looking down into your face and wondering what kind of woman you'd grow up to be. I'm proud of you, Susie."

Susan smiled at her mother's use of the old nickname. "Thanks, Ma. That means a lot to me."

They climbed the stairs together, each going off to their own room to sleep.

~

IT WAS RIGHT at seven when Lucy pulled the wagon in front of Harriett Long's house the next morning. "Do you want me to wait and give you both a ride to the station?"

Susan shook her head. "No, I think we'd both rather walk. It's a beautiful morning."

"Do you have your sandwiches?"

"Yes, Ma." She patted the lunch pail she had beside her on the wagon seat. "I'll be fine. I promise."

Lucy pulled her in tightly for a hug. "You be careful on that train, and don't forget, you're welcome to come back home if things don't work out."

Susan knew she'd never come home. She'd find a job if she had to, but she wouldn't go back to living with her parents. This was goodbye. "Bye, Ma. I love you."

"I love you, too."

Susan climbed down and grabbed her things. Between her bag, purse and lunch pail, she wasn't sure how she was going to knock on the door, but she'd be okay. She was ready to be on her way.

She set her carpet bag down and waved goodbye, before turning to walk up the sidewalk toward the Long house. Harriett must have been watching out the window, because she had the door open before Susan reached it. "Are you ready?" Harriett called.

Susan nodded and smiled. "As ready as I'll ever be."

Harriett held up a package wrapped in brown paper. "I made you some sandwiches for the trip."

Susan laughed. "I think my Ma made me seven of them." She held her lunch pail up for Harriett to see.

Harriett grinned taking Susan's lunch pail from her to make her burden lighter. "We'll add my five, and you'll have an even dozen. You may be sharing with everyone around you to get them eaten before they go bad."

"It'll be easy to make friends on the train with so much food to share!"

They walked toward the station together, Susan having to move slowly to make accommodations for Harriett's awkward gait. The station was only a fifteen minute walk from Harriett's house, and they passed the time with Susan explaining how much sewing they'd done to get ready for her to marry. "I thought I'd just wear my new green church dress for the wedding. Do you think that'll be okay?"

"Since you're not having a formal wedding that will be perfect. And remember, Jesse said he'd have a sign with your name on it. That should make him easier to spot."

"I remember." They'd reached the station and sat down to wait for the train to be called.

28

"There's one thing I like to talk to my brides about before they go," Harriett began hesitantly.

"What's that?"

"I want you to know that once you're married, you can still leave if you find yourself in a bad situation. All you have to do is contact me, and I'll send train fare for you to come home."

Susan made a face. "My mother keeps telling me not to feel the need to stay if the situation is bad. Just come home. This is your business, and even you think it's a bad idea for me to go?"

Harriett shook her head. "I don't think it's a bad idea. I think this is opening up marital choices for young women and making it possible for them to see places they never would have been able to see. I just worry I'll send a woman to a bad situation, and she'll need to get home and will feel stuck."

"Have you had any complaints?" Susan was truly startled by the conversation. It was almost as if Harriett was trying to tell her not to go.

"Well, I've only had the business for a few months, but so far, everyone has been happy." Harriett paused as she studied the younger woman's face, hoping she was listening. "I do ask that you send me a letter once you arrive to let me know you're safe, and another a few weeks after marriage. I want to make sure you're still happy once the first meeting excitement has passed."

"I'll write as soon as I get there and again a few weeks later. I'm not going to be a victim for any man."

"Many women feel like they have no choice once they've married. They think they're required to stay no matter what." Harriett leaned forward in her seat, her face earnest. "I don't want any woman I send out to be in a bad situation and feel like she has no option but to stay, because you always have options."

Susan nodded. "I promise." She wasn't sure whether she'd promised to get Harriett to back off, or because she already knew what Harriett was telling her. She didn't believe a woman should have to stay in an abusive relationship and never had.

Harriett looked relieved, and started to say something else, but it was cut off by the conductor's cry of "All aboard!"

Susan hugged Harriett quickly. "Thank you for the sandwiches and all your help. I'll write as soon as I arrive." She figured she'd write the letter on the train to make things faster. As soon as she arrived in Fort Worth, she'd drop it at the nearest post office.

"Be safe."

Susan grinned. "I will!" She took her things and stood in line for the train. Her first train ride. What could be more exciting?

~

TEN DAYS LATER, Susan knew that riding on a train wasn't anything to get excited about. She was tired, dirty and ready to get off. The woman sitting across from her had two young children, and Susan had slept with one of them across her lap. She couldn't seem to get away from children anywhere. She was ready to be married and living in a home with no small children.

She looked down at Johnny, the sleeping young boy on her lap. He was two, and had been motion sick during a lot of the trip. Susan knew she had some vomit on her shoulder. She'd been so proud of how she looked in her new pink dress when she'd left Beckham. Now she wished she could bathe before actually meeting Jesse. What would he think of how she looked when she got off the train?

"I'm sorry he threw up on you," his mother, Sally, said softly as if she could read Susan's mind. They'd been traveling together since St. Louis and had become fast friends.

Susan smiled. "I'm used to it." She'd already told Sally about being the oldest of twelve children, so she knew the woman would understand.

"You certainly have a knack with him." Sally cradled her infant daughter in her arms. "I think we're close. Are you nervous?"

"More disgusted with myself than anything. I wish I could take a bath before meeting Jesse."

"He'll understand. Ten days on a train will leave anyone worse for the wear."

"I hope so." She'd been so sure of herself when she'd left Beckham, but every mile the trains had taken her closer to Fort Worth, she'd become more and more nervous. She prayed Harriett had been right about Jesse having a bath ready for her when she arrived, and she thought she'd try to stay downwind of her future husband until she had that bath.

The conductor walked through the train car then calling out the next stop. "Fort Worth, Texas coming up! Fort Worth, Texas!"

Susan took a deep breath. "That's me." She settled Johnny onto the seat beside her, careful to make him comfortable before standing up and getting her bags from where she'd stowed them under her seat.

"I hope you find every happiness with Jesse."

"Thank you. I wish you were stopping here too!" It would have been so much easier to get off the train knowing she had a friend living close by.

"You have my address?"

Susan nodded. "I'll write to you soon. I promise." She

stepped into the aisle of the train and made her way out, stopping just before getting off to wave goodbye to her new friend.

She stepped off the train onto the busy platform and looked around. There was no one holding a sign with her name that she could see. She moved a little still looking. Finally, she spotted him. *Oh, I wish I'd had a way to fix my appearance before meeting him!*

She raised her hand and waved and made her way through the terminal. He matched the description he'd given her exactly. He was tall with dark hair and brown eyes. "Hi, Jesse! Forgive the way I look and smell. Ten days on a train is hard."

The man smiled down at her and took her bag from her, putting one hand beneath her elbow to guide her. "Let's find a bench to sit down and talk." The serious look on his face had her frightened.

"Is something wrong? You didn't find someone else to marry did you?" His face was so serious, she immediately worried something had happened.

He found a park bench a block from the train station and invited her to sit. "I'm not sure how to even start…."

Susan sighed. "Just spit it out. Please. Whatever it is, we'll deal with it." Susan had received bad news, and she found it easier if she just found out quickly and then was able to make the plans she needed to make. Prolonging things just drove her crazy.

"I'm not Jesse. I'm his brother, David."

"Not Jesse? Was he delayed at work?" Why would Jesse send his brother to meet her instead of coming himself? Had he decided against marrying her?

David sucked in a breath, his Adam's apple bobbing as he fought for control. "Jesse was killed two weeks ago in a shooting in Hell's Half Acre."

"Killed? Hell's Half Acre?" Susan was stunned. She'd just traveled over a thousand miles to marry a man who was dead? She didn't have money to get home. She had enough for a night or two at a boarding house, but then she needed to find a job and fast. Where could she find a job?

"He was doing a story of a murder in Hell's Half Acre. The Acre is an area in Fort Worth where the brothels and saloons are. He would never have gone there if he hadn't had to for a story. He was really excited about meeting you." David spoke quickly.

Susan knew she should grieve Jesse, but frankly, she'd never met the man. She was grieving the life she had imagined having with him. Finally, she collected her thoughts. "I'm sorry for your loss." *But what am I going to do?*

David nodded. "Thank you." He paused for a moment, looking at the girl beside him. He'd come planning to ask her to let him take Jesse's place, but the shock on her face made him wonder if that was smart. "Let's find you a boarding house for tonight, and we'll talk about some options for you." He stood and picked up her bag. "I made arrangements at a small boarding house to the south of town, because I live down that way. My buggy is this way." He led her through the streets to the buggy parked in front of a lawyer's office. "I had to talk to him about Jesse's affairs this morning."

Susan wondered if there was enough to pay her fare home for a brief moment, but then decided no matter what, she was staying. Surely there was someone somewhere who needed a cook or maid. She wasn't above working for a living. "Okay."

He helped her into the buggy, and she stared straight ahead, wondering what she could possibly say to the man sitting beside her. "I have a proposition for you if you want to hear it."

She turned to him quickly. "A job?" *Oh, please have a job for me. I don't want to go back and live with 'the demon horde'.*

He shook his head. "No, more of an arrangement."

She sighed. "I need a job." She turned to face the front of the buggy again.

"Well, maybe not. You see, after Jesse told me he'd sent off for a mail order bride, I decided I'd do the same thing. I was about to send off for a wife myself. Would you be willing to marry me instead of Jesse?"

Her eyes widened. "I don't know anything about you." Of course, she'd met him and she'd never met Jesse. She already knew him better than she ever knew his brother who she was planning to marry.

"Honestly? I'm a lot like my brother. I'm a Christian. I'm twenty-eight years old. I'm a rancher. I inherited our parents' spread a few years ago."

Susan's mind worked rapidly. Would it be so bad to just marry him? Sure, she'd planned to marry another man, but he was dead. She couldn't marry him, and since she'd never met him, she wasn't exactly in love with him. The man beside her was handsome, and seemed intelligent enough. "Why haven't you married already if you're twenty-eight?"

"I did. She died in child birth two years ago." His voice sounded hollow.

She looked over at him. He'd had so much loss in his life. His parents, his brother and his wife? "The baby?"

"The babies were fine."

Babies? "Twins?" She had younger brothers who were twins. Did she really want to deal with two year old twins?

"Yeah. Both boys."

Boys. Could she be an instant mother to two boys? It certainly wasn't the situation she'd wanted, but she was good with children. "Are they well behaved?"

He shrugged. "They're two. I don't really know if there's another way to answer that."

She sighed. There really wasn't. Two year olds were just two. They had their good moments and their bad. "Would it be okay if I met them before I make my decision?"

He looked surprised, but nodded. "Of course. Why don't I pick you up at the boarding house and have you over for dinner tonight?" He pulled the buggy to a halt and jumped down. "I'll be here around five if that's okay."

She had no clue what time it was, but guessed it couldn't be much past noon. She'd have time to eat lunch, get a bath and maybe even a nap before going out there. "That sounds fine."

He carried her carpet bag to the house and knocked on the door. A woman who looked to be in her sixties came to the door. "Ah, Mr. Dailey. Is this the lady you told me about?"

"Yes, ma'am. This is Susan Miller. Susan, this is Mrs. Duckworth."

Susan smiled. "It's nice to meet you."

"Come in. Come in." Susan stepped inside, but was surprised when Mrs. Duckworth stopped David. "Not you. This is a ladies' boarding house."

He nodded. "Okay. I'll leave her with you then. I'll see you at five."

"Five," Susan agreed. As soon as he'd closed the door behind him, Susan looked around. The house was clean and the furniture of good quality, although worn. "Is it possible for me to take a bath?"

Mrs. Duckworth nodded. "I was going to insist."

Susan laughed. "I've been traveling for ten days. A little boy vomited on me on the train. Repeatedly."

Mrs. Duckworth made a face. "I can smell that." She turned and led the way up the stairs. "I'll show you your room, and then bring the tub up for you."

"Thank you so much. I promise, I don't usually look or smell this way."

"I'm happy to hear it." Mrs. Duckworth smiled at Susan. She showed her the room. "Your first two nights have been paid for. We'll work out what to do after that."

The room was small, but adequate. There was a single bed, dresser and a small mirror. "This will be perfect for me. Thank you."

Susan waited until Mrs. Duckworth had left the room before collapsing on the bed and burying her face in her hands. How could her perfect wedding day have dissolved into the kind of mess she was facing?

CHAPTER 3

*B*y the time David returned at five to take her to dinner with his family at his ranch, Susan had bathed and washed her hair, eaten lunch and taken a nap. She was dressed in her new lavender dress with her hair back in a tight bun that she hoped made her look older than eighteen. She wanted the boys to immediately see her as an authority figure, because if she decided to marry David, she needed to have their complete respect from the first day. It wasn't terribly important with the twins being so young, but she wasn't going to risk making a weak first impression.

She waited for him on the front porch, amazed at how hot it was. She'd never felt heat anything like what she had felt since stepping off the train. There was a slight breeze, but not really enough to cool her down as she sat in the rocker watching for David.

He came alone and jumped down from his buggy to help her up. "You didn't have to wait outside."

She laughed a little. "I was hoping to catch a breeze if I sat on the porch, but there wasn't much breeze at all."

"I know it's hot. You'll be thankful come winter, though,

because our winters are very mild here. We get snow only once or twice a year if that." He walked around the buggy to get in beside her. "We have running water in my house as well, so you can take a cold bath during the day to cool down if you want to."

She turned to stare at him. "Running water? Really?" Susan had never even seen running water, let alone used it. At home they hauled the water from the well, and used the outhouse. Running water was a true luxury.

"I had it put in as a wedding gift to my wife."

"What was her name?" She wanted him to feel like he could talk about his late wife to her anytime he wanted, so she asked a question to let him know the subject was open.

"Caroline."

"How did you manage newborn twins without a wife?"

He shrugged. "I hired a round-the-clock nurse for them." He didn't add that they'd always used nurses for the boys. He didn't want her to marry him because of the material things he could provide. He honestly wanted a woman who would be a good wife to him. He didn't think she cared about his wealth because she'd agreed to marry his brother who had come right out and told her she would have to live frugally for at least the first few years of marriage, but he couldn't be too careful. Of course, none of the women in the area would marry him even though they knew how rich he was.

He'd had a long talk with the boys before leaving the house that evening telling them they were to be on their best behavior while Susan was there, and he would give them each a dollar. He told them how important it was to him to get a new wife and that they'd better not mess things up.

"How far is it to the ranch?" she asked, feeling more nervous than she'd expected to. She was relatively certain she'd end up married to him, just because she was in a situation that required her to make quick decisions. She didn't really want to be an instant mother, but if it was her only choice, then she'd do it in a heartbeat.

"It's about five miles. The drive takes right at thirty minutes."

"That far?" Somehow she'd expected him to live in the city like his brother, although she realized that was ridiculous. How could he be a rancher in the middle of the city?

"Will you be upset to be away from the city?"

She shook her head. "Not at all. I wasn't looking forward to living in the city. I've always lived on a farm, so that's what's familiar to me." She really didn't think she'd like city life. Living in the country was something she'd always enjoyed.

"Really? A farm? I didn't realize. I never read your letters to Jesse, so I don't know what you told him."

Susan nodded. "We had a few horses, some cows, and lots of chickens, but we were mainly crop farmers. I assume you raise beef cattle?" From what she'd read about Texas, beef was one of the primary exports.

"Yes. I also have a side business where I train horses and sell them. It's not the moneymaker the cattle are, but I enjoy it a lot more."

"How did you get into that?" She wasn't sure what to say to him, and she found asking questions about others made for lively and interesting conversations.

He shrugged. "I've actually been training horses since my parents were alive and owned the ranch. It was my own business that I used to make money. After my parents died, I made it a part of the ranch." He looked over at her and smiled. "The boys love the horses. I think Albert may end up following in my footsteps and being a horse trainer."

She laughed. "You can't tell that much about their personalities at two."

"Albert's my eight year old."

She turned to stare at him in shock. "Eight year old? I thought you had two year old twins?"

"I do. I have an eight year old, a six year old and two year old twins."

She swallowed hard. Four of them? He'd only mentioned two! "All boys?"

"All boys." He sighed. "We were hoping for a girl the last time. Caroline really wanted a daughter."

She wanted to insist he turn the buggy around and take her back to the boarding house immediately. She couldn't do that, though. She had nowhere to go really. She sighed. "Four boys." Could she deal with four boys? Were they both wasting their time?

He gave her a surprised look. "You don't like boys?"

She shrugged. "I don't *not* like boys. I was really hoping to not be an instant mother, though. Four boys is a lot to take on."

He needed her to change her mind. He needed a wife and a mother for his boys before he went through every nanny in the state of Texas. "Will you meet them before you make your decision?"

She nodded reluctantly. She really didn't feel like she had a choice in the matter. "I'll meet them."

He took her hand in his and squeezed it. "I'll make you a deal. If you don't want to marry me, I'll pay your train ticket home, no questions asked."

She turned to him in surprised. "You'd really do that?" She couldn't fault his generosity. He didn't know her, and he didn't have to agree to do something like that for her.

David nodded. "But you have to agree to give my kids a chance. They're good boys." *Deep down somewhere, there's good in them. No, I'm not being fair. They* are *good. They're just a lot more active and rambunctious than most women like to see.*

He pointed out his property line as they passed it, and she

stared at the open expanse of prairie land. There were barbed wire fences that came up to the road, and she could see a herd of cattle grazing in the field. "Wow, so many of them. And all yours?"

He laughed. "This is one small portion of the herd. I keep them divided up into ten sections for grazing."

Her eyes opened wide in awe. She'd gone to Texas to marry a struggling newspaperman, and she was being offered the opportunity to be the wife of a rich rancher. If money meant anything to her, she would jump on the chance. In fact, she knew a lot of girls who would marry him just for his wealth, but she wasn't one of them. She would judge him on his own merits.

It was a full five minutes before he pulled up in front of a large white wooden house and parked. The house was as big as any she'd ever seen. Harriett Long's house had certainly been more elegant, but it wasn't any bigger than David's house.

He walked around the buggy and helped her down, handing the reins off to a man. "Unhitch it for me. I'll let you know when I'm ready to take her back to town."

"Yes, sir." The young man was around her age and obviously was one of David's employees. Her family farm was just that. A family farm. Every member of the family who was old enough worked hard to keep it going. David obviously employed people to keep his ranch working for him.

David slipped his hand beneath her elbow and led her up the three steps to the front porch. The porch was huge and went around the house. There was a porch swing along with several rocking chairs. Her feet were mauled by three black and white puppies as she stood there. Giggling, she crouched down to stroke their heads. "They're adorable."

"We're just keeping one. We're looking for homes for two of the others."

41

She stood up. "I love dogs. We've had several back home." She wondered if any of them had been painted lavender since she'd left.

He opened the door and said a silent prayer that all would be well. He'd left Mrs. Hackenshleimer, the boys' new nanny, in charge and she seemed to be a no-nonsense type woman. She'd raised five boys of her own and now was more than willing to take on the task of other people's children.

Mrs. Hackenshleimer had the boys sitting on the couch, all formally dressed and looking out of place. She walked to the door and held her hand out for Susan. "I'm Ada Hackenshleimer," she said in her thick German accent.

Susan smiled at the woman. She was tall, and round, with dark hair and dancing brown eyes. "Are you the boys' nanny?" The woman nodded at her. "I'm Susan."

"It's nice to meet you, miss." She turned to David. "Would you like me to stay this evening?"

David thought about it for a moment, and decided to keep her there for the evening. She had a calming influence on the boys because she hadn't been their nurse long enough for them to find her weak points. "Yes, please. Will you have dinner with us?"

Mrs. Hackenshleimer shook her head. "Absolutely not. I'll eat in the kitchen with the rest of the staff. I'll be out as soon as you're finished dining."

David was afraid to argue with her pronouncement. She intimidated him as much as she did the boys. He wanted to say, "Yes, Ma'am" as she left, but that last time he'd done that, she'd told him to stop being cheeky, so instead he watched her disappear into the kitchen. He could hear her tell Sadie the cook and housekeeper who had been with the family since before he was born that the family was ready for dinner.

David took Susan's hand and introduced her to the boys.

"This is my oldest boy, Albert. He's eight. Next to him is Lewis. He's six. Then the twins are Thomas and Walter. Thomas is the red head and Walter is the blond." He pointed to each boy as he introduced them.

She smiled down at the four of them all looking up at her expectantly. "It's nice to meet you all. I'm sorry to hear about your uncle." She hadn't decided yet if she was more sorry for them or for herself, though.

Albert nodded solemnly obviously the spokesman for the four boys. "We really miss him. He was our only relative other than Pa. I sure hope you'll decide to stay and be our ma."

"Well, I'm here to meet you and we'll decide." She looked at the boys trying to memorize their names quickly. She noted that the two older boys both had dark brown hair like their father, while the twins were lighter. Albert and Lewis looked so much like their father it was startling, while the twins had a totally different look. *They must take after their mother*, she thought.

They all turned at the call of dinner from an older woman. Susan watched her as she placed the food on the table. If she wasn't a relative, then who was she? Surely he didn't have two servants in the house!

David saw Susan's confused look and introduced her. "Sadie, this is Susan. She's the woman I told you about. Susan, this is Sadie. She's been with my family since before I was born. She runs this house, although she lets me think I do."

Sadie put the platter of fried chicken on the table. "Don't you try to sweet talk me now, David. I already made your favorite dessert. There's nothing else you need from me." She turned and went back into the kitchen.

Susan could see that the table had already been set and they were just waiting for her and David to arrive to put the food on so they could all eat. Sadie emerged from the kitchen again with a huge bowl of mashed potatoes and another of gravy. Then she went to the kitchen to return with a bowl of green beans and some bread on a wooden board shaped like a paddle.

Susan smiled at Sadie. "That all looks delicious. I've been eating train food for over a week. A home cooked meal will do me a world of good." She truly was thankful to have food other than sandwiches to eat.

Sadie looked Susan up and down. "You're too thin. You need to eat up. If you come live with us, I'll do my best to fatten you up."

Susan laughed. "I don't know that I need fattening, but I appreciate the gesture." David held out a chair for her at the foot of the table and she took her seat, trying to act as if she were seated by a man every day, but feeling very awkward.

The boys each sat two to a side. The twins had taken the seats beside their father who was obviously used to helping them with their meals. Albert and Lewis sat on either side of her, calmly waiting for the prayer before they fixed their plates. Susan was impressed. Her brothers would have fallen on the food like rabid dogs.

David smiled at Susan. "Let's all hold hands as we thank God for the meal."

Susan's left hand found Albert's while her right hand joined with Lewis's. She bowed her head while David said a quick prayer thanking God for sending Susan into their lives. Susan felt her eyes tear up as she listened to it. His boys seemed so well behaved and he obviously wanted a wife so badly. If nothing went wrong, she knew she'd agree to marry him on their trip back into town.

They passed the dishes very politely around the table with the older boys helping the younger boys with their portions. Susan was amazed. She could easily take on the boys if they were always this well behaved.

She took a bite of her mashed potatoes with the cream gravy. "This is wonderful! Do you always eat so well?"

David nodded. "Sadie is the housekeeper and the cook. If you'd like to cook meals, you can always let her know you'd prefer to cook a certain night, but she's used to cooking for all of us. The ranch hands have their own cook and live in the bunkhouse, so they never intrude on our family time unless there's some kind of emergency I need to know about."

Susan took a moment to think about that. She wouldn't even have to cook? And there was a nanny for the boys? What would she do with her time? "What do you need a wife for? You have a nanny, a cook, a housekeeper. Would I just sit around and file my nails all day?"

He laughed. "I do have four boys. There need to be two women working together to take care of them. Caroline did a lot of charity work as well. And you'd do all the sewing for us and the mending. Caroline used to say the sewing itself was a full time job."

She nodded, thinking about the life she'd have as his wife. She turned to Albert. "I hear you love horses."

Albert turned his big brown eyes to her and nodded. His whole face was lit up by his favorite subject. "I do. I want to train horses like my pa. Someday I'm going to train the fastest horse in all of Texas!"

"Not in all of the United States?"

"If it's the fastest horse in Texas, it *is* the fastest horse in all of the US!"

She laughed. "You're not proud to be a Texan are you?"

Lewis poked her arm from her other side. "Of course, he's proud to be a Texan. If you're not a Texan, you're nothing!"

"Well, I think it's a good thing I moved here then!"

The boys regaled her with tales of the Alamo among other stories from when Texas was a republic. She was amazed they knew their history so well.

She watched as the twins ate their meal. They had horrible table manners, but she expected that from two year olds. She could work with them on that.

Once the meal was over, the boys all went into the parlor and she followed. The parlor was next to the dining room with an open archway in between. David was right behind her with his hand at the small of her back. "Would you like a tour of the house?"

She turned and smiled at him over her shoulder. "Yes, please!"

"This is the main parlor. If we have guests over, we usually come in here with them." He took her elbow and steered her down a hallway. "This is our washroom." He opened the door and she saw a small seat with a pull chain. "That's our water closet." Next to it was a large claw foot bathtub with two knobs above it. She assumed they were to adjust water.

He led her to the next room and it was another smaller parlor. "What's this room for?"

He shrugged. "We use it more as a family gathering room. The boys play here a lot, and Caroline used to do needlework in here." He ran his hand over the back of a blue sofa that had seen better days.

Susan liked this room better than the formal parlor at the front of the house. The furniture was older and the rug on the floor was faded, but it felt a lot more homey than the formal parlor. She could see herself sitting there with the twins playing at her feet. "I really like this room."

He smiled. "The boys love to play in here."

She could see a box of wooden blocks in a corner of the room pushed up against the wall. There was also a bookcase along one wall with old worn books that had obviously been read and loved. Susan loved to read when she had time, so she liked the idea of exploring them all.

He led her up the stairs and showed her the boys' bedrooms. The two older boys shared a room and the two younger boys shared a room as well. The rooms were tidy, but not spotless, just like a boy's room should be. She ran her hand over the dresser in the twins' room. There were small beds that were low to the ground with quilts covering them. "Do the boys like sharing rooms?"

"It's all they've ever known. They don't really need to share, because we have two spare bedrooms, but I think it's good for them to learn to get along at a young age, and learn they can't have everything they want when they want it."

She nodded in agreement. He showed her the two spare bedrooms which were perfectly made up and ready for occupants. He pointed to another room, and said "My room's through there." She just nodded and headed for the stairs to go back down.

"Where do Sadie and Mrs. Hackenshleimer live?" She asked over her shoulder as she descended the stairs.

"There are two small rooms on the other side of the kitchen. That's their portion of the house. There's another small bathroom over there for their use, and the family uses the one on our side." He gestured toward the kitchen which she hadn't seen yet.

"May I see the kitchen?"

"I don't think you'll spend much time in it, but sure." He led her through the dining room, and she saw the table had been cleared off and the dining room cleaned. Walking through the door on the other side of the dining room, he showed her the kitchen.

It was huge, and had a small table for four people as well as a modern cook stove with a coal bin beside it. There was a sink with running water and cabinets lined the walls. "This is a beautiful kitchen," she told Sadie who was standing at the sink with her hands in dishwater. "May I help you finish?"

Sadie shook her head and shooed them toward the door. "This is my job. You go have fun with the family."

Susan sighed. "I'm used to doing dishes for a large family. I'm happy to help anytime." She didn't want anyone to think she was afraid to get her hands dirty with household chores.

"When I decide to go off and spend a week with my son's family in a few months to help when his wife has a baby, you're more than welcome to cook and clean to your heart's desire. For now, I'll do the dishes."

"I'll take you up on that," Susan said with a smile.

She followed David out of the kitchen and back to the formal parlor where Mrs. Hackenshleimer was sitting with the boys. The twins were sitting on the floor playing with small wooden trains while the older boys were sitting on the couch taking turns reading a book aloud to one another.

Susan's younger brothers went on a literacy hiatus during the summers and refused to open books at all. She was very impressed with the young Dailey boys and knew she'd tell David that on the way back to Fort Worth. She'd seen what she needed to see. She would marry him if he still wanted her.

She smiled over at David. "Would it be okay if I went back to the boarding house now? I haven't slept in a bed except for my thirty minute nap today in over a week, and I'm exhausted."

David nodded turning to Mrs. Hackenshleimer. "I'll be home in an hour and a half or so. Thanks for working late this evening."

"It's never a problem."

Susan smiled at the older woman. "It was nice meeting

you." She waved fondly at the four boys. "Thanks for having me over for dinner tonight," she told them.

David opened the door for her and led her outside. He signaled to the young man who had unhitched the team earlier that it was time to get the buggy ready to return to town. He took her hand and helped her down the steps so she wouldn't fall in the setting sun. She was amazed at just how beautiful the sunset looked over the Texas prairie.

"It's beautiful here."

He nodded. "I can't imagine living anywhere else."

She grinned at him. "I noticed your boys were very proud of being from Texas."

"Only because I raise them right, ma'am." He winked at her as he said the words.

She shook her head and sighed. "Will I always be considered inferior around here because I'm not a native Texan?"

"Well, you can't become a native if you weren't born here, but you got here as fast as you could, and that'll have to do."

The buggy was led in front of them and he handed her up. He walked around and climbed in beside her taking the reins. "Thanks, Sam. Go on to bed. I'll unhitch the team myself when I get home."

"Okay, boss." Sam tipped his hat to Susan before David moved the buggy away and down the long driveway leading to the road.

David rested his arm across the back of the seat against Susan's shoulders. "So what did you think of my boys?" He said a silent prayer thanking God they'd been so well-behaved that evening. Bribing the older two with a dollar each to spend however they wanted had certainly worked. He'd never seen the two boys voluntarily pick up a book in their lives.

She smiled at him. "They were very sweet and well behaved. I was expecting hellions like my own younger siblings and was very pleasantly surprised. You've done a good job with them." She folded her hands together in her lap watching the darkened road as they drove back toward Fort Worth. "Would Mrs. Hackenshleimer stay on if we were to marry?"

"Absolutely. She knows the boys' routine and I think it's better if she sticks around to help them with the transition."

Susan breathed a sigh of relief. She really didn't think his boys would be a lot of work, but knowing they wouldn't be released into just her care immediately made her feel a lot better about accepting his proposal. "I think that's good."

He looked at her out of the corner of his eye, hoping against hope she'd made the decision he so badly wanted her to make. "So do you think you can join my little family and be a mother to four boys?"

She bit her lip, wondering if she was making the right choice as she nodded. "Yes, I'll marry you."

With an excited yell, he pulled the buggy off to the side of the road and turned to her. "Thank you! You won't regret it." He used the arm across her shoulders to pull her toward him. "I think all engagements should be sealed with a kiss, don't you?"

Her eyes widened. She hadn't expected that. "I guess…."

"Trust me on this. I've been married before and you haven't." He cupped her face in his hands looking down into her green eyes in the moonlight. His thumb traced against her bottom lip.

She stared up at him, enthralled by the look in his brown eyes. She'd never been kissed before, and being touched by a male who wasn't a member of her family was completely foreign to her. His thumb against her lip sent a shiver down her spine that surprised her. Then his head was lowering toward hers and her lashes fluttered closed.

The first brush of his lips against her was as gentle as a

butterfly's wings. His lips just barely touched hers. When his lips came back for a second brush against hers they were less tender and more demanding. He pressed them hard against hers, his tongue tracing the seam of her lips and asking for entrance.

She parted her lips to ask what he wanted, and his tongue gained access before she could get any words out. At the first stroke of his tongue against hers, she was startled. She hadn't known people kissed that way, but then she opened her mouth further to give him access. His kiss was causing a tingling right down to her toes she couldn't help but enjoy.

Her hands rose to his shoulders and clung to him. It felt so very strange to be in a man's arms, but so good at the same time. She'd worried about what her wedding night would be like with a man she barely knew, but the way he was making her feel let her know her worries were unfounded. He knew exactly what he was doing and would make everything right.

After a moment, he lifted his head, his dark eyes staring down at her in the darkness. "I want to get married tomorrow," he whispered.

She nodded. "I thought today would be my wedding day, so that's fine." Her mind was sluggish and she tried to think. "Are we going to marry at the courthouse?"

"It'll be faster that way." He brushed her lips one last time with his before turning and picking up the reins again. "Do you mind if the boys attend the wedding?"

She shook her head. "Of course not. They're well behaved, so I don't see that being a problem at all." She could picture how sweetly they would sit with their hands folded in their laps paying attention to the vows.

He took her hand in his and held it for the rest of the drive to the boarding house. "Why don't I pick you up around ten in the morning, and we'll go to the courthouse to speak our words? I'll get Sadie to cook up a nice wedding lunch for us, and I'll have a few of the area ranchers and their wives over so you can get to know a some people before you settle in."

She leaned back against the seat and stretched a bit. "That would be nice. Just not too many people. I'm too tired to have to play hostess for a big party. One night's sleep isn't going to be enough after that long train ride."

He pulled up in front of the boarding house and helped her down walking her to the front door. "I'll keep it to five or six of my closest friends and their wives." He noticed Mrs. Duckworth had been kind enough to leave a lit lantern on the front porch for Susan. He brushed his lips against hers and opened the door for her. "I'll be here at ten. Have your things packed and ready to go."

"I'll be waiting for you."

She stifled a yawn as she went inside and closed the door behind her. Mrs. Duckworth went to the door to see who was there. "Is that you, Susan?"

"Yes, ma'am."

Susan had explained a little about her situation earlier in the day, and Mrs. Duckworth was understandably curious. She knew little of David Dailey, but she had thought he was a kind enough man when he'd reserved the room for Susan the previous day. "So what did you decide?"

Susan blushed. "He's picking me up for the wedding at ten tomorrow morning."

Mrs. Duckworth smiled. "We'll start getting you ready as soon as the breakfast dishes are done, then. I know you just had a bath today, but we'll get you another, and I'll fix your hair for you if you'd like."

"Oh, I don't want to take you away from the other things you need to be doing."

"I never had a girl. Only boys. I'd love to help a young

lady get ready for her wedding. Will you let me play mother for a few hours tomorrow?"

Susan laughed softly and nodded. "Thank you. I'd like that very much."

"Go and get a good night's sleep. With a husband and four boys to deal with, this may very well be your last full night of sleep for a long while."

Susan didn't tell the woman how angelic her future step-sons were. She didn't want to brag too much. "Good night. And thank you."

～

WHILE SUSAN BATHED after breakfast the following morning, Mrs. Duckworth ironed the dark green dress Susan had made for the wedding.

By the time Susan was out of the tub and wearing her petticoats, Mrs. Duckworth had her dress ready. "Do you know how you want your hair for the wedding?"

Susan shook her head. "I've worn it in braids and in a bun all of my life. I've never even looked at other hairstyles. At home, it was all about what was the best way to keep it up and away from your face so you could work."

Mrs. Duckworth walked in a circle around Susan who was standing in the middle of the room with her hair piled on top of her head to keep it from getting wet during her bath. "Take your hair down so I can see how long it is."

Susan pulled the pins she'd put in it to keep it up, and her blond hair cascaded down her back like a waterfall. It went to the back of her knees. She stood still as the older woman eyed her. "What do you think?"

Mrs. Duckworth smiled when she saw all the hair and gave a quick nod. "I know just what we'll do." She waved to the straight back chair she'd brought up to the room earlier. "Sit. We need to get started."

Susan sat down and stared straight ahead as Mrs. Duckworth went to work on her hair. She brushed it out little by little, and once it shone, she began the elaborate up-do she had in mind. While she worked Susan asked her questions about her life to fill the silence.

"You said you only had boys. How many did you have?"

"Only three. I wanted an even dozen, but the good Lord knew I couldn't possibly handle that many once my husband died." There was a note of sadness in the older woman's voice as she mentioned her husband.

"When did he die?"

"Well, let's think. I was twenty five when he died so it must have been thirty eight years ago. He died in the Texas War of Independence. I didn't want him to fight, because I was pregnant with my third at the time, and had a six year old and a three year old, but he was filled with pride for his homeland. He couldn't stand to let Santa Anna's troops take over, so he fought." The woman stopped and wiped a tear from her eye before resuming her task of fixing Susan's hair.

"I'm sorry. It must have been really hard for you to raise three boys on your own."

Mrs. Duckworth nodded. "This house was all I had back then. I put the two older boys in a room together, and when the baby was born, he shared with me. I started taking in boarders. Just two to start with, but then I realized I could easily handle more. Now I have up to six boarders at any given time."

"Do your boys visit often?"

"Oh, they're all right here in Fort Worth. My oldest is a banker. He keeps trying to get me to close the house and move in with him, but I like my independence. He has two teenage sons. Then the middle one owns a saloon." She shook her head. "I hate it that he works in The Acre, and I tell him every time I see him. He never married."

"And the youngest?"

"He's a preacher. Married to the sweetest girl I've ever met, and they have four little ones. The oldest is twelve and the youngest is two. I love having my grandchildren near me." She paused as she stuck another pin in Susan's hair. "They come over for Sunday dinner every single week."

"That must be nice for you. Do the older boys come for dinner?"

"Of course, just not so often. I find I'm closer to my youngest. Maybe because he never knew his father at all."

"I wish I was staying here long enough to meet them all. It sounds like you have a lovely family."

Mrs. Duckworth stepped back and nodded. "I wish you were too. I'd love for you to meet them." She made a slow circle around Susan checking her work. "It's perfect." She picked up a hand mirror she'd brought in and handed it to Susan. "What do you think?"

Susan moved the mirror around looking at her hair from different angles. "It's wonderful. I love it." She jumped to her feet and hugged the older woman. "Thank you so much!"

Mrs. Duckworth smiled. "I'm happy to help. Your mother can't be here for your special day, so someone has to stand in for her." She turned to the bed where she'd laid Susan's dress. "Let's get this dress on you. You did a beautiful job on it."

"Thank you. My mother and I decided it made more sense to make a practical dress for the wedding so I could wear it to church on Sunday as well."

"Very smart. I never saw the need of making a special dress you'd only wear once in your life. This will be a very serviceable church dress." Mrs. Duckworth helped Susan put the dress on so it wouldn't disturb her hair. She walked around behind her and buttoned her up to the top button.

"You look very beautiful. The green really brings out the color of your eyes."

Susan wished there was a way to see her entire body in a mirror, but she had no way to do that. "Does it fit okay?"

"Absolutely. It shows off your figure to its best advantage as well. Your waist looks tiny in that dress."

Susan sighed. She hated how tiny her waist looked in comparison to the rest of her body. Her waist was supposed to be small, but her breasts were so large, they made her waist look like it wasn't real. "What time is it?"

"You have about fifteen minutes before he gets here. I guess we need to pack up the last of your things."

At ten, she was waiting in the parlor with Mrs. Duckworth. She tried not to stare out the window, but it was hard. Her new family would be there any minute to pick her up.

When they pulled up, she stood and smoothed her dress down nervously. She picked up her bag and smiled at Mrs. Duckworth. "Thanks for everything. I couldn't have asked for a better mother to help me get ready."

Mrs. Duckworth laughed. "It was my pleasure."

"Are you sure you won't come for the wedding?"

"I really can't. I have to get lunch ready. If I'd had more notice, I'd have called in a friend to fix it for me, but twelve hours just wasn't enough."

"I understand." She went to the door and opened it. "I'll come visit you soon."

"I look forward to it!"

David was on the front porch waiting and took her bag from her. "I'll put this in the back of the buggy."

She followed him down the steps and to the buggy. The boys were sitting in the back with Mrs. Hackenshleimer who had both twins on her lap. David handed her up and they made the short drive to the courthouse in silence.

Once he had parked the buggy, he came around and helped her down. "You look beautiful today."

Susan blushed. "Thank you." She turned and took the twins one at a time from Mrs. Hackenshleimer and set them on the ground. As soon as Mrs. Hackenshleimer was down, she took each of the twins by the hand and walked with them toward the courthouse.

Susan walked behind her with David, the older boys on either side of the couple. "Are you nervous?" he asked.

She nodded. "I've never been married before."

"Well, I have, and it's nothing to be afraid of. The ceremony will be simple, and then we'll head out to the ranch." He just hoped the boys could behave for long enough to have her legally tied to him before she realized they were hellions. Mrs. Hackenshleimer had a firm grip on the twins' hands and she'd watch over the older two during the ceremony. He was almost there.

They entered the courthouse and went to the judge who was waiting for them. David had sent a messenger in that morning that he'd be there at ten and needed a few minutes of the judge's time. The ceremony was short and simple, and Susan was surprised when the judge pronounced them husband and wife. It was so short, it didn't seem like it could possibly be legal.

After he'd kissed her briefly, they all trooped back out onto the street. Susan looked at David. "That was so fast. It doesn't feel like it could possibly be real."

David smiled and stroked her cheek. "It's absolutely real. You are now Mrs. David Dailey."

She once again found herself mesmerized by his brown eyes. What was it about this man that brought out strange urgings inside her? She didn't know, but she was glad she had feelings for him. It would make marriage so much easier.

Susan heard the howl of a cat, and turned to see one of

the twins had a cat by the tail. The cat broke away and ran down the street. Both twins tore free of Mrs. Hackenshleimer and ran after the cat. The older boys took off after the twins.

Within moments Susan watched the twins fall off the boardwalk and into a puddle of mud created by a store owner dumping a bucket of mop water. They stood up dripping mud. Their Sunday clothes were covered and they were howling with anger because the cat had gotten away.

The older boys were still running after the cat and dove toward it, bonking heads on the way down. The cat streaked away, but Albert and Lewis shouted at one another.

"I can't believe you let her get away!" Albert yelled.

"It's all *your* fault! I had her!" Lewis pushed his brother.

Not ten minutes after her wedding, Susan watched her two youngest step-sons howling in the street dripping mud while her older boys fought with their fists not twenty feet away.

One of the shopkeepers came out of his store to see what the commotion was. He sighed. "Oh, it's just those rotten Dailey boys again." He shook his head as he went back into the store.

Again? Susan's heart sank. She'd married a man who came with hellions. She glared at David. "Again?"

David met her eyes and shrugged innocently. "This may have happened once or twice before."

Susan marched to the buggy and climbed up with no help. He could deal with his own children. She refused to deal with monsters within an hour of her wedding. When they arrived home would be soon enough.

CHAPTER 4

Susan was silent while David and Mrs. Hackenshleimer rounded up the boys and for the trip back to the ranch. She couldn't believe David had deceived her, but really, what had she expected from a stranger? Sure, he was a stranger she enjoyed kissing whom she was now married to, but he was still a stranger.

She watched the scenery pass by wondering what to expect from her wedding lunch. She was not looking forward to having to appear happy and hosting a large group of people with the mood she was in. Her wedding day was ruined, and she was in the same situation she'd been in back home, except now she was expected to be the parent. How could she have misread the family so badly?

When they pulled up in front of the ranch, David helped Susan down from the buggy and led her into the house. He turned to Mrs. Hackenshleimer. "Will you see to the boys, please? I think I need to spend a minute or two talking to my wife before our guests arrive in thirty minutes." He put his hand under her elbow and led her up the stairs to his bedroom, putting her bag on the bed.

She glared at him. "I'm not sleeping in here with you." She honestly couldn't believe he'd expect her to with the way he'd deceived her. What was his problem?

His eyes narrowed dangerously. "What do you mean?"

"Do you really think I'm going to sleep with you after you deceived me? I don't want more children who will behave like the ones you've already got." She folded her arms across her chest, letting him know she wasn't backing down.

"You're their mother now. Discipline them and turn them into good kids. They were better behaved when their mother was alive." He moved toward her, standing over her and glaring down at her. "And you're sleeping with me. You're my wife."

She refused to back up, even though he was doing his best to intimidate her. "You're okay with me disciplining those boys as I see fit?" She poked him in his chest. "And I'm not sleeping with you. I'll sleep in one of the spare bedrooms."

"I don't believe in hitting children, but short of that, discipline them however you want." He caught her hand and held it behind her back. "And you *are* sleeping with me. You're my wife and you belong in my bed. If you don't want to consummate the marriage, fine. But you're sleeping in my bed."

"That's just stupid! Those boys need to be beaten with a switch!" She kicked at him. "And there's no reason for me to sleep with you when there are two empty rooms right across the hall."

"What is wrong with you? You think you need to beat my boys and kick me? Violence will get you nowhere in this house!" He bent down and crushed his lips to hers, forcing a response from her. When he raised his head, his brown eyes stared into hers. "You *will* be sleeping with me whether you think it's stupid or not. I won't have Sadie knowing my wife is sleeping in another room."

"Fine! You can sleep on the floor." She tore herself from

his arms, and turned her back to him, pressing her fingers against her lips. Why did she like it so much when he kissed her, even when he was rough about it?

"I'll sleep beside you in the bed." He walked up behind her and put his hands on her shoulders. "I'm sorry if you feel like I deceived you into marrying me. I haven't been able to find a wife thanks to the boys, and I saw you as my only chance."

She turned to face him. "Why didn't you send off for a mail order bride yourself? A lot of women wouldn't mind being saddled with an instant family."

He shrugged. "I was going to, but after Jesse died, the situation seemed too good to pass up." He ran his hands up and down her arms. "I need a wife and my boys need a mother. And you needed to find a job or a husband. You have a husband now."

She sighed and shook her head. "Fine, but I'll be your wife in name only. Nothing is going to happen between us that could possibly create a child. I'm already going to have my hands full with the hellions you already have." She wasn't about to mince words with regard to his son's behavior. If he didn't like it, he shouldn't have hidden their true nature from her before they married.

He winced when she called the boys hellions, but he knew she was right. They were awful. "That's fine. Just don't shame me by sleeping in another room, please."

"I won't." She hated to give in to him, but she could understand a man's pride and need to save face.

He glanced at the clock sitting on the dresser. "It's time to go down and greet our guests."

She shrugged. "I guess we need to go then." She looked at him. "I hope you realize I'm furious with you."

He nodded. "I know. And I *am* sorry."

She followed him out of the room and down the stairs to where their guests were already starting to assemble. The boys were all freshly scrubbed and dressed in clean clothes. The clothes weren't as nice as the ones they'd worn to the wedding, but they would have to do. Albert had a fat lip and Lewis's eye was starting to swell. She took the boys by the hands, and said, "Excuse me," before she was even introduced to any of the guests. She didn't much care if David thought she was rude. She needed to handle her new sons.

She took the boys back to the family parlor at the back of the house and glared at them. "Do you two really think fighting is appropriate? On my *wedding day*?" Her emphasis on the last two words was meant to fill them with guilt, and by the looks on their faces, it worked. They both shook their heads looking up at her with wide eyes. "What do you have to say for yourselves?"

They both hung their heads, not saying a word. It was obvious they didn't know how she'd react and were doing their best to act contrite. She'd seen the same looks on her brothers' faces over and over. "The first part of your punishment for fighting *on my wedding day* will be holding hands until every guest is gone. That means at the table, while you're playing, and whatever you do, you will hold hands. Do you understand?"

Albert looked up at her to protest. "No way! I'm not going to hold his hand!" He poked his brother in the arm to emphasize his words.

Susan shook her head and stepped forward to intimidate the boy. "You will, and you'll do it with a smile. For every time I see you drop hands during the party, you'll write twenty times during play time tomorrow, 'I love my brother.'"

"You can't make me do that!"

"Oh, yes I can. You *will* behave, and you will start now!" Susan knew that if she let them get away with fighting on her wedding day, they'd always think they could run all over her.

It wasn't going to work that way. She was their mother now, whether deception had been used or not, and she would see to their discipline if it killed her. "Do you both understand me?" The boys nodded, and she watched as they joined hands. "Let's go join the others."

She made the boys lead the way so she could watch and see if they dropped hands. She walked back to the front of the house and joined David who was talking to a man and his wife. David saw her slip up beside him and raised an eyebrow at her in question of what she'd done. She simply shrugged and smiled at the woman across from her. "Hi. I'm Susan."

The woman smiled as she noted the boys holding hands and looking miserable. "I'm Beverly Smith. We have the ranch that shares your south border." Beverly was a petite red head with a pretty smile.

"It's very nice to meet you. Do you have children?" Susan engaged Beverly in conversation, asking her questions about herself and watching the boys out of the corner of her eye.

"I have three girls. They're six, four and two."

Susan noticed the boys drop hands. "Excuse me for just a moment," she muttered and strode over to the boys. "That's your first twenty sentences each. How long do you think it will take you to reach one hundred?"

The boys quickly joined hands again, and she walked back to Beverly and her husband. "Sorry. I need to let them know who's in charge."

Beverly laughed softly. "Those boys have needed someone to let them know who's in charge for a long time." She squeezed Susan's arm. "You're going to be very good for them."

Susan smiled. "Either that or I'll kill us all trying to turn them into well-behaved boys. They *can* behave. I've seen it. So they will." The look in Susan's eye left Beverly in no doubt that she would have the boys behaving like little gentlemen within a month.

"I really think I'm going to like you. Would you like to come over for coffee and cookies one afternoon next week? After you've had a chance to settle in? Maybe Wednesday?"

"I'd like that a lot. It'll be nice to have a friend in Texas. Maybe it'll help me not be so homesick." As soon as the words were out of her mouth, Susan realized she really was homesick. She missed her parents and Elizabeth a lot. She needed to sit down and write them a letter as she'd promised.

"Where are you from?"

"I was raised on a small farm outside of Beckham, Massachusetts. It's different here."

"I was raised in Pennsylvania, so I know what you mean."

"How long did it take you to get used to the scorching heat?" Susan asked as she rubbed her hand along the back of her neck to wipe away the sweat that was pooling there.

Beverly shook her head. "I don't think you ever get used to it. You learn to bear it, but that's all you can expect of yourself."

"How did you end up in Texas?"

"My husband was travelling and he came into a restaurant I worked in as a waitress. He sat at my table and I served him lunch. He was lonely, and asked if I'd show him around town. When he left town I left with him as his wife."

Susan smiled. "I like that story. How long did you know one another before you married?" Beverly's story was certainly more romantic than her own. She'd shown up ready to marry and her bridegroom was dead so she'd settled for his brother. No, there wasn't much romance in her story.

"Three weeks. My mother was not happy with me."

Susan laughed. "Imagine how my mother felt when I said I was moving across the country to marry a total stranger."

"I'm surprised they let you go."

Susan shrugged. "I'm the oldest of twelve. I've always been very independent, and I think they knew if they tried to stop me, I'd leave anyway." She realized then the men had stopped talking and were listening to them. She looked at David.

He took her hand and smiled down at her as if there were nothing wrong between them. "Charles, this is my wife, Susan. Susan, my closest friend and our closest neighbor, Charles Smith."

"It's nice to meet you," Susan replied. She noted that Charles was tall, although not as tall as David. He had blond hair and blue eyes. He wore a cowboy hat with his suit. She wondered if all men did that here, because David had worn the same thing for their wedding. They both wore cowboy boots as well.

Charles nodded at her, his hand slipping around his wife's waist. "We'll have to get together sometime soon. Find a night when your nanny can stay with your boys, though. I don't need your wild boys around my sweet girls."

"I'm really hoping Susan will have a calming influence on the boys," David told him.

Susan looked around, realizing she hadn't seen the boys for a minute or two. Finally she spotted them off in the corner with the twins and Mrs. Hackenshleimer. Their hands were still linked, and she smiled. "I hope so too. I'm not going to be able to put up with their shenanigans for long."

Charles grinned. "I can't say David, Jesse and I were any better when we were boys." He looked at David. "Do you remember when your mother banned us from ever playing together again? What had we done that time?"

David's face lit up with a smile. "I think that was the time we tied the two cats' tails together and then threw a bucket of water on them." He laughed out loud. "I'll never forget the sound those cats made."

Susan shook her head in disbelief. No wonder the boys were so bad. They took after their father. She saw Sadie waving to her from the dining room and quietly excused herself to go talk to the housekeeper.

"Lunch is ready."

Susan nodded. "Thank you, Sadie. I know this is going to seem odd, but for today, will you serve the boys in the kitchen? The two oldest have to continue holding hands even while they eat."

Sadie's eyes widened and she grinned. "I heard they were fighting in the street on your wedding day. That's a fitting punishment."

"I'd prefer to take a switch to them, but David says he won't allow that, so I'll just have to get clever with my punishments." The narrowing of Susan's eyes left Sadie in no doubt that she was up for the task.

Sadie rolled her eyes. "I think the boys need a switch, but David feels like it's cruel. His mother never used one, so he doesn't think they're good for boys. His boys would be much better behaved if he used one, though."

Susan smiled, thrilled to have an ally. "Would you let me know if they stop holding hands? I have a backup punishment in case they do."

"I'll let Mrs. Hackenshleimer know to watch for that. I'll be serving lunch."

"That's fine. Thank you, Sadie. Why don't you start loading the table and I'll call everyone to eat when I see it's mostly full?" Susan had never had a servant before, so it seemed strange to her to ask the older woman to do things for her, but Sadie made it easy to work with her.

"That sounds good. We're not doing anything formal, just steak and baked potatoes served with butter. I made some beans and a wedding cake as well."

"It sounds delicious. I'll send the boys to the kitchen now."

She walked to the corner where the boys were sitting with Mrs. Hackenshleimer. Her eyes drifted deliberately to the older boys' joined hands, before she asked Mrs. Hackenshleimer to eat with the boys in the kitchen. "I won't always have the boys eat in the kitchen, but until I've had some time to teach them how they're now expected to behave, I'd rather keep them out of the way of humans."

"I'd be happy to." Mrs. Hackenshleimer stood and took the twins by the hands to lead them from the room. The older boys followed automatically.

Once the four boys were out of the room, she announced that lunch would be served in a few minutes, before rejoining David. Another couple had joined their circle and she was introduced to Anthony and Jane Vandergriff. Jane had dark hair and pale blue eyes. She wore an ice blue silk dress that matched her eyes perfectly, and seemed to think everyone in the room was beneath her. Susan didn't bother to try to strike up a conversation as she had with Beverly.

David guided Susan to the foot of the table and pulled her chair out for her. She smiled as Beverly took the seat next to her. David sat at the head of the table directly opposite her, which thrilled her. She wouldn't have to make much conversation with him that way, and she found she was still seething over his deception.

Susan barely picked at her meal, eating no more than a few bites. The food was delicious, but she simply didn't have an appetite. The four couples David had invited for the meal obviously knew one another well and they all talked and joked while they ate. Susan spent most of her time observing them.

She already knew she liked Beverly, but Jane was someone

she had no desire to get to know. One of the other women seemed to snub Beverly and only talked to Jane. Susan had yet to meet her, but she had dark hair and brown eyes. Susan made a mental note to avoid her. The last woman of the group sat to Susan's left, and seemed very quiet. She was in the same age group as all the others, around her mid-twenties, but she was plump and plain. Her mousy brown hair seemed to be forever falling from her bun and her eyes were brown.

Susan smiled at her. "I'm Susan."

The woman seemed surprised to be singled out. "I'm Wilma."

"It's nice to meet you. Which of these men are you married to?" Wilma pointed out the man Susan had seen her with earlier. He was a tall blond with startling good looks. "Do you have any children?"

Wilma shook her head. "Not yet. We've only been married a few months, though."

"How did you meet your husband?" Susan had always loved to hear stories of how couples met and married. Each story had filled her with a sense of hope for herself when she was single, and now it was a habit to ask.

"I've known him all my life. My father and his father were best friends. I think I've always known that I'd end up married to Ned. He's been off fighting the Indians in New Mexico with the Cavalry, but as soon as he came home, he started courting me."

"We'll have to get together sometime so you can tell me more about it," Susan encouraged.

"I'd like that."

Beverly smiled. "You should join Susan on Wednesday and come to my house for coffee around two."

Wilma looked at Beverly with a surprised look. "I'd love to. Thank you."

By the time the guests had left for the day, Susan was

exhausted, but thrilled she'd made two new friends. She was finding the Texas women to be easy to get to know. Her mind drifted to Jane and the other woman she hadn't bothered to get to know.

After they'd all gone, she looked at the two older boys. "How many times did you drop hands? And remember. I was watching."

Albert and Lewis exchanged looks. Finally, Albert said, "Just twice."

She'd only seen it happen once, but was thrilled they told on themselves. "Then you know that before either of you go outside to play tomorrow, you'll be sitting at the table writing forty sentences for me, right?"

"But I don't know how to spell," Lewis whined.

"I'll write it for you once, and you can copy it." Susan didn't think it would hurt the boys to sit and write forty sentences before they went outside.

David walked up behind her. "What's this?"

Susan turned to him. "I told the boys they had to hold hands the entire time the guests were here today. For every time they dropped each other's hands they have to write twenty sentences about loving their brother for me." Her eyes dared him to argue.

David nodded slowly. "That sounds like a fitting punishment for fighting."

"Why were you boys chasing that cat anyway?" Susan asked. Not that it mattered to her punishment, but a reason for their behavior would help her understand them better

Lewis shrugged. "We wanted a cat."

Susan sighed. "Maybe if you asked your father, he'd get you a kitten."

Albert looked at David in surprise. "Would you, Pa?"

David thought it over for a moment. "I don't know why not."

"The cat will be your responsibility, though. You'll feed it and give it water. I will not be taking care of a cat, when I have you four boys to take care of." Susan's voice was firm, and both boys nodded eagerly.

"We'll do it!" Lewis said with excitement.

Sadie came into the room then. "I've made sandwiches for supper. I didn't think you'd want more after the big lunch."

Susan nodded. "That sounds lovely." She walked to the table and was surprised when David seated her once again. She'd thought he was only doing that to impress her and their guests. Maybe he really did have manners.

The boys all sat down and bowed their heads while David prayed over the food. She watched as the boys wolfed down their meal. Shaking her head, she knew table manners would have to be one of the first things she worked with them on.

After dinner, Sadie cleared the table while Susan got the twins ready for bed. She enjoyed the little boys and was happy to change them into their pajamas and tuck them into their little beds. She kissed each boy on the cheek and left their room quietly.

The bigger boys were sitting in the family parlor talking to their father. She waited outside the door listening for a moment before going in.

"We don't want to have to write sentences," Albert complained.

"I don't care what you want. You'll do what your new mother says, and you'll do it when she says. You've been running wild for too long, and you'll obey her. Do you understand that?"

"Yes, Pa," Lewis said.

"Yes, Pa, but I won't like it." Susan stifled a giggle at Albert's belligerent tone.

Susan walked into the room. "Go on and get ready for bed," she told the boys. "You'll be writing your sentences before you do any playing tomorrow." She sat down on the sofa and folded her hands in her lap.

The boys jumped up to go get ready for bed, obviously afraid of another punishment coming their way.

"Thanks for backing me up."

David nodded. "I do know they're monsters. I just don't know what to do about it, short of beating them, which I'm not going to do."

"Well, I honestly wish you'd let me use a switch on them, but since you won't, I'll find another way to get them to behave. I'm not going to have our lives in constant chaos just because those boys don't feel like behaving. They obviously know how. Now it's just a matter of enforcing some ground rules."

David eyed her doubtfully. "If you say so." He stood up stretching his neck. "Would you like to go for a short walk before bed?"

She looked at him skeptically, but then nodded. "That sounds nice." She did want to see the ranch. The few times she'd been outside had been brief. She enjoyed being outdoors, and wanted to know what was out there.

He walked her around the yard, pointing out the different buildings and explaining their functions. "The ranch hands live there. No women are allowed in there under any circumstances."

She nodded. "Sounds like a good rule. Do you let the boys go in there?"

He shook his head. "Not without me."

"You'll have to let me know about rules like that. I think I'm going to make up a rule board for the boys and let them know what the punishment is for each thing. That way they know what they're getting into if they break a rule."

He took her hand in his. "I appreciate you jumping in so quickly to help get the boys under control."

She sighed and shook her head. "It's my job now. I don't think the twins are going to be a problem. They're still so young; they'll just learn to obey me. The older two are the ones I'm worried about."

"Don't be worried about them. I don't think there's going to be a problem. You seem to have it all under control." He stopped to lean against a wooden fence at the front of the house pulling her to him with the hand he held. "Would you consider making our marriage a real one?"

She sighed staring up at him. "I really don't want to bring another child into this situation. I can't imagine having a newborn and dealing with your hellions." She wasn't trying to be cruel with her words, but she needed him to know where she stood.

He used his forefinger to tilt her face up to his. "Our hellions."

"Our hellions." She watched as he slowly lowered his head toward hers, brushing her lips gently with a kiss. Her hands moved up to his shoulders and she clung to him, almost afraid she'd fall over. There was something about his kisses that left her weak in the knees.

"We'll have the boys under control well before a baby comes along," he whispered against her lips.

She shook her head, pulling away. "My mother was always so sick with morning sickness she neglected the discipline of my younger brothers and sisters. That's why I'm the oldest member of a family whose children are referred to by the city of Beckham, Massachusetts as 'the demon horde.'"

He stifled a laugh. "I promise you, if you get pregnant, I'll follow through on all your rules and discipline the boys exactly how you think they should be disciplined. Without the switch, of course. I won't use a switch."

"How about a belt? Or paddle?" She grinned as she suggested the alternatives that would work just as well.

He grinned. "No beating. Any other punishment you can devise is fine."

"Would you build a dungeon?" She tilted her head to the side to ask the question. She would never put children in a dungeon, but it was interesting to see just how far he'd go.

He laughed out loud. "You really don't like children, do you?"

"I love children. Ill-behaved children need to dangle from trees by their toes until they learn the correct behavior."

He caught her hand and pulled her back into his arms. "Fix my boys for me." He lowered his head to hers, his tongue reaching out to trace her top lip. "And go upstairs with me and be my wife."

Once again her hands clung to his shoulders. She was his wife, and she knew as his wife, it was her job to let him consummate the marriage. Besides, she liked the idea. She'd enjoyed kissing him and wanted to see what came next. "Okay."

CHAPTER 5

*H*is head came up and he looked into her eyes. "Really?" She nodded slowly, and he started tugging her toward the house as if he didn't want to give her a chance to change her mind.

She laughed softly. "Are you always in this kind of hurry?"

He didn't stop as he answered, simply pulling her along toward the front door. "It's been over two years. You bet I'm in a hurry." He flung the door open and pulled her up the stairs and into their bedroom. He quickly sat on the edge of the bed and removed his boots, and then knelt before her, untying her shoes and slipping them off her feet.

He rose to his feet and stood before her trying to force himself to slow down. He had to keep saying over and over in his head that this was her first time, and he couldn't be in such a hurry with her.

She stood looking at him by the dim light from the moon drifting in through the window. Her mother had talked to her about the way things happened between a man and his wife before she left, but it hadn't made her any less nervous. Of course, she'd been raised on a farm, so she'd had a pretty good idea of what went into making babies anyway.

He shut the bedroom door and took a step toward her. "Turn around so I can unfasten the buttons on your dress."

She obeyed, turning around and presenting him with her back. "I'll need to get my nightgown."

"No, you won't. There's no need for a nightgown in the summer. It's too hot for that nonsense." He quickly unbuttoned each of her buttons, pressing quick kisses to the back of her neck, and turned her around to face him. He pushed the dress off her shoulders and down to the floor. His fingers went to her hair and plucked out each of the pins that held her hair in place. He ran his fingers through her hair his eyes widening as he saw the length of it.

Once she was standing in just her petticoat, he leaned down and kissed her, his tongue immediately demanding entrance to her mouth. She opened for him, and moved her hands to his shoulders while he kissed her. Her hands went to the buttons on his shirt and slipped them out of their holes. She pushed his shirt off his shoulders and down to the floor.

She thought she'd be more embarrassed about standing in just her petticoat in front of him, but the relief of the slight breeze coming through the window was almost worth it. She wished she could throw cold water over both of them, but was certain he'd think she was insane.

He continued to kiss her as he dropped his hands to the waistband of his slacks and unfastened them before dropping them and his underwear to the floor. He stepped out of his slacks and pulled her to him, his manhood pressing against her petticoat.

She was shocked to feel him against her, but knew it was a part of being a wife, so she said nothing. His lips went to her shoulder, and he moved the strap of her petticoat aside to give himself better access to her bare skin. Soon she felt him push the other strap down and he dropped her petticoat to the floor.

"You have a beautiful body," he whispered.

She blushed. "I'm glad you like it." He pushed her backward until the bed hit the backs of her legs and then toppled her over onto it. She let out a quick laugh. Somehow she'd pictured him picking her up and carrying her to the bed, not pushing her onto it.

He followed her down, propping himself on one elbow as his hand moved over her bare breast. "Are you laughing at me?"

She shook her head. "At myself more than anything. I just never pictured my bridegroom pushing me onto the bed. I guess I always thought I'd be carried and gently placed there."

He grinned. "My way is faster and more fun." His fingers plucked insistently at her nipple.

"I think it is." She looked down and watched his fingers playing with her nipple in the dim light of the moon which shone through the open window. It was strange to watch him touching her that way, but oddly, it sent tingles through her, making her much more aware of his strength as opposed to her softness.

His lips went to her neck and bit her gently. "That feels nice," she whispered.

"Tell me if there's anything you don't like."

She laughed. "So far that's just not happening."

His hands traced her hips and went straight down to the curls that shielded her innocence. He smiled at her surprised gasp, and moved his fingers down between her legs, which were clenched tightly together. "Spread your legs for me, sweetheart."

She moved her legs slightly apart and his fingers went immediately to her core, one of them slipping quickly inside her. She hadn't expected him to touch her there with anything but his man-part, so she jerked in surprise. "What are you doing?"

"Don't worry. You'll like it." His finger slipped in and out of her slowly at first, but gathering speed. "I want you to be ready to accept me."

She swallowed hard, knowing what he was referring to. His fingers did feel good, and they seemed to be pushing her toward some unseen goal that she didn't quite understand. She looked at his face in the darkness and saw an intense look in his eyes, almost as if he was in pain. Her hand reached up to stroke his cheek as his finger played inside her.

After a moment David turned his head and brushed a kiss across the palm of her hand. He moved his finger out of her, and before she had a chance to protest, he had slipped it back in with another finger added. She moaned softly with surprise and pleasure. She'd had no idea this part of marriage would feel so good. She'd expected to simply lie back and submit to her husband, but she wanted so much more from him.

She felt like she was getting close to something, and started to move her hips with his fingers, thrusting back against them. "That feels so good," she whispered.

David took that as his cue and removed his fingers and rolled over so he was resting between her thighs, but catching his weight on his elbows. "This should feel good too then." He dropped his lips to hers and kissed her passionately just as his member pushed against her opening.

She was startled to find him on top of her and pressing against her so quickly and his manhood felt nothing like his fingers had. She'd never seen a fully erect penis and was surprised at the size of the thing pressing against her. She moved her hips a little to give him better access, because she believed him. She'd loved everything he'd done to her so far, and she was looking forward to having him deep inside her.

When he felt her move against him, he knew it was time, and pressed deep inside her, breaking her barrier on the way. He held still when she let out a startled cry and stared up at him in the dark.

She wiggled her hips trying to get more comfortable, but it wasn't working. It still hurt. "It doesn't feel good. Your fingers were much nicer." She knew she should just lie back and submit to him, but it hurt and he'd said it would feel good. Had he lied to her?

He groaned as she wriggled beneath him. It was all he could do to hold still while she adjusted to his invasion of her body, but her movements were just adding flames to his already burning libido. "Stay still for a minute while the pain passes."

"I can't. It hurts." She kept moving under him, her hips driving against him and moving from side to side trying to escape the pain.

After a moment, he gave in and started to thrust inside her driving them both toward their pleasure.

He wasn't able to hold out as long as he'd hoped, because it had been so long, and it was just moments before he let out a groan and collapsed on top of her.

Susan lay beneath him disappointed. After the initial pleasure when he had used his fingers, she'd hoped for more. Toward the end it hadn't hurt as badly, but there had been nothing spectacular at the end like she thought there would be.

She sighed heavily, and he opened his eyes looking deep into hers. "You didn't enjoy that very much, did you?"

"Not really. Sorry." And she was. She'd hoped to enjoy it. A friend of hers at church had whispered to her all about how much fun being a wife was, and she'd expected a lot more of the experience.

He rolled to her side, stroking her cheek. "You'll like it more next time."

"Okay." She said no more, but it was obvious by her tone of voice that she didn't think she would.

He rolled to his back and pulled her against him, pillowing her head on his shoulder. "I promise. It'll get a lot better."

She snuggled into his side already closing her eyes. She was surprised she was able to get so comfortable with a man in her bed, but she was so tired, she just needed to sleep. It had been an exhausting, emotional day, and she had a battle ahead of her training the boys to act the way she expected.

He stared down at her wondering what to say, but realized she'd already fallen asleep. He smiled. His new wife was so much more than he'd expected her to be. Her spirit would keep him on his toes.

CHAPTER 6

*T*he next morning after breakfast, Susan sent the twins off with Mrs. Hackenshleimer and sat down with the two older boys. "We need to talk for a few minutes before you start writing your sentences." She'd set some paper and two sharpened pencils on the table for them to write with.

Both boys looked at her with wary eyes as if they were expecting to hear something they didn't want to. They were right. "We're going to set some rules for the house, and you will follow them. If you don't there will be consequences."

Albert sighed and glared at his brother as if it was his fault they were having this conversation.

"The first rule," she said pulling a piece of paper to her so she could write each rule as they discussed them, "is no fighting. Never for any reason should brothers fight each other. If someone hits you, you may hit them back to defend yourself, but you never hit your brother for any reason. Is that understood?" Her eyes darted back and forth between their faces as she waited for them to answer her.

Both boys nodded. Lewis folded his arms across his chest. "He started it."

Susan sighed and shook her head at them. "I don't care who starts it. If I see you two fighting again, I'll tie your hands together for an entire day so you won't be able to do anything without learning to work together."

Albert nodded. "Yes, ma'am."

"The second rule is always display good manners. Last night at supper you two acted like ravenous wolves who hadn't eaten in months. I know that wasn't the case. You know how to eat correctly, and from now on, you will. I don't care how hungry you are, you will eat with your mouths closed and you will say please and thank you at the table."

Lewis made a face. "What happens if we don't?"

She hadn't thought of a consequence for that, so she sat and thought about it for a minute. "You'll be limited to bread and water for the rest of the meal and your next meal. You'll get to eat whatever the rest of the family is eating as long as you've shown good manners at the previous meal." She thought that sounded like a fitting punishment for bad table manners.

Albert's jaw dropped. "There's no way Pa would let you do that!"

"Your pa told me to teach you to act right. He told me I can do anything I want." She didn't add that he'd told her not to spank them. She didn't want them to know that wasn't something in her arsenal. "The third rule is always obey the first time. If I tell you to get your brother a glass of water, I don't want to be asked why you have to do it, or why he's thirsty. I just want it done and done correctly. Do you understand?"

Albert sank into his chair as if he'd been slapped. "What's the punishment for that one?"

"I'll make you repeat the action ten times. So if you don't get your brother water, or question why he needs it, you'll make ten trips back and forth to the kitchen with glasses of water." She watched their faces as she told them the punishment.

Lewis put his head down onto the table. "Are we ever going to get to have fun again?"

Susan laughed. "All the time. You'll find following the rules makes life a lot more fun for you, because you won't be in constant trouble." She stood up. "I'll be adding more rules as we go, but those are the three we're starting with. Go ahead and write your sentences." She walked toward the kitchen, expecting them to obey her automatically after their talk.

"I don't know how to spell those words, remember?" Lewis made a face at her.

Susan nodded. She walked back to the table and handed him the paper she'd already written the sentence on for him. "Forty times each."

She slipped into the kitchen and found Sadie cooking a large pot of beans for lunch. "Have they always been this way?"

Sadie grinned at Susan. "They were good boys before their mother died, but having an endless stream of nannies here and no one to really take charge made them think they didn't have to follow rules at all. I'm glad you're taking charge the way you are."

"Why did the nannies leave?" Susan was almost afraid to ask, but as their new mother, she needed to know.

"The last one left because the boys kept putting frogs in her bed. The one before that left because they threw eggs at her while she was playing with the twins outside. So it was for a lot of different things, but they all had very good reasons." She paused and looked at Susan. "I think you're doing the right thing by punishing them right away."

Susan fixed herself a glass of water from the pump in the kitchen and leaned against the work table. "I just hope it works. Not being able to spank them takes away a lot of my power." She shook her head in disgust at the way her hands were tied.

"Just stay strong. They'll obey."

Susan pushed the door open a crack to see if the boys were working.

"She can't make us write the sentences, you know." Albert's voice came through loud and clear.

"Are you sure?" Lewis asked.

"Positive. I mean what's she going to do if we just get up and go outside?"

Susan walked into the dining room. "How are the sentences coming along?"

Albert stood up. "I've decided I'm not going to write them."

Susan set her glass of water on the table and put her hands on Albert's shoulders forcing him to sit. "You will write them, or you won't play at all today."

"You're not my mom! You can't make me."

"I'm not your mom, but I am your step-mom and the only mother you'll ever have. You'll sit there and do the work, or you'll never play again. I guarantee I can stand over you all day if I have to."

Lewis looked at her stubborn face and knew she meant business. He bent his head and immediately started to write the sentences. He wrote quickly and carefully made each letter.

Albert, on the other hand, sat and stared at her as if he was sure she would just let him go if he continued to refuse. He stood up and she pushed him right back down in the chair. Lewis finished and went outside to play while she stood over Albert waiting for him. He still hadn't picked up his pencil to write a single word.

Susan spoke very quietly. "If you don't pick up your pencil and start writing by the time I count to three, I'll double the sentences. And you will spend the rest of the day in your room once you're finished writing them." She took a deep breath. "One." She looked out the window and smiled as she saw Lewis running along the edge of the fence line as if he was racing the brown mare on the other side of the fence. "Two." Albert picked up his pencil and started writing. He did it grudgingly, glaring at her the entire time, but he wrote. Within twenty minutes, he was finished.

Once he was done, she sat next to him at the table. "I know you don't want to obey me. I know you think I'm the enemy, but I'm your father's wife, which makes me your new mother. I can be your best friend in the world, or you can make me your worst enemy. Either way, you'll act the way I want you to act. I will not give in. Your behavior will improve if it kills both of us." She stood and picked up her water glass walking back into the kitchen. "Have fun outside, Albert."

She was leaning against the counter in the kitchen when she heard the door slam. Her eyes met Sadie's and Sadie began to laugh. "This is going to be fun to watch!"

SATURDAY WAS Mrs. Hackenshleimer's day off, and Susan braced herself for the onslaught when she woke up. She helped the twins eat their breakfast, and then went outside with all four boys to watch them as they played. She took some mending with her so she could sit in the shade of a tall oak tree while watching them.

It wasn't long before she started to hear squeals from the pig's pen. As she rounded the corner, she saw that all four boys were in with the pigs chasing a small piglet who was running from them and squealing loudly. The twins were covered in mud. She could see it oozing out of their diapers as they ran. The two older boys had mud all over their faces and in their hair.

Instead of going over to stop them immediately, she instead headed for the well, and pulled up a bucket of ice cold water. She carried the water over to the pig pen, but the boys were so involved with chasing the pig, they didn't notice her. She took careful aim, and threw the entire bucket of freezing water at Albert and Lewis, knowing they were the ring leaders and the twins were just following suit.

The boys sputtered and screamed. Albert glared at her. "Why did you do that?"

Susan studied the belligerent boy for a moment before saying, "Well, since you were in the pigpen getting filthy, I knew you must want to take a bath, so I thought I'd help you out." She set the bucket on the ground and then lifted Thomas and Walter over the fence and led them into the house. "You boys go ahead and keep splashing in the mud. Once I have the twins bathed, I'll come for you and get you washed as well."

"You can't give me a bath! I don't want you seeing my privates!" Albert yelled after her.

Susan shrugged still walking away. "You'd better be clean before I'm done with your little brothers then." She didn't care how much it upset Albert. He'd either clean himself with the water from the well, or he'd take a bath with her there. It was his choice.

She took both little boys into the bathroom and stripped them down to their birthday suits. Even their little stomachs were completely covered with mud. She ran water into the bathtub for the first time, and put them both in. She knelt by the side of the tub washing their little bodies tenderly, talking to them the whole time. "Your big brothers are going to get you into trouble if you keep listening to everything they tell you to do. What were you trying to do anyway?"

"Give piggy bath," Walter told her.

"Why would you want to give the piggy a bath? Piggies like to be dirty." Susan was sure one of the older boys had told them to do it, but she wanted to hear them say it.

"Bert said piggy needed bath," Thomas said.

"I see. It was Albert's idea? Did he tell you to help?" Had he deliberately coerced his two year old brothers into the pigpen or had it been their idea?

Walter gave her a very serious look. "Bert said we could play if we caught piggy."

"Of course he did. Let me give you two a little piece of advice. Your brother Albert is trying to get you two in trouble." She soaped up their hair and washed them down. "You need to stop listening to him."

She lifted first Walter and then Thomas from the tub. She rubbed them both dry and led them up the stairs totally naked to their bedroom. She put clean diapers and shirts on them, but no pants. It was too hot for them wear pants anyway. Taking them back downstairs, she went into the kitchen to Sadie. "Can you feed these two while I chase down the other two and show them who's boss?"

Sadie nodded taking Walter and putting him in one of the high chairs they kept in the kitchen. Susan lifted Thomas into the other chair. "Wish me luck."

Sadie grinned. "Good luck. I wish I could see this one."

Susan went to the bathroom and refilled the bathtub before she left the house and walked back toward the pigpen. It only held pigs, and she noted the piglet the boys had been chasing was still there. She looked around for the older boys.

Finally, she spotted Albert as dirty as ever, leaning against the corral. She walked slowly, hoping to have the element of surprise on her side. She grabbed Albert's arm just as Lewis spotted her. "Lewis, follow me." She half dragged Albert into the house, leading both boys into the bathroom. "Lewis get undressed and into the water. Albert? You do the same."

Albert folded his arms across his chest and shook his head. He made it very clear he wasn't about to get undressed in front of his step-mother. She started counting very slowly. When she reached three, Lewis was sitting in the tub washing himself, but Albert was still glaring at her. She reached out and unbuttoned his shirt with him kicking and screaming and wiggling to get away from her. "Stop it! You can't take my clothes off! You're a girl!"

"Take them off yourself then. You're getting in that bath-tub, and you're getting in there now." She folded her arms across her chest to give him a chance to do it himself. "One." She looked down at Lewis who was staring slack jawed at her battle with his older brother. "Two." Albert unbuttoned his pants and stepped out of them, turning his back to her before removing his drawers and jumping into the tub with his brother. He kept his hands covering his penis as he looked up at her and glared.

"Get clean. You have ten minutes, and I'll be standing outside the bathroom the entire time." She left the bathroom, but stayed close enough she would be able to hear whatever they were doing. She did give them privacy, though.

David came into the house and saw her standing in the hallway outside the bathroom. "What are you doing?" he asked as he dipped his head and gave her a quick kiss.

"Having another battle of wills with our eldest son." She looked at him to see how he'd react to the situation.

"Who's winning?"

"The same person who will always win. Me."

David bit back a laugh. "What's this one about?"

"Albert convinced the others that catching a piglet and giving him a bath was a good idea. By the time I heard the pig squealing, the twins had mud oozing out of their diapers and the only things you could see of their faces were their eyes and mouths. I told Albert I'd bathe the twins and come back for him and Lewis." She briefly explained how she'd caught Albert as he was leaning against the corral and forced him to undress. Her eyes were twinkling as she said, "He really didn't want me to see his 'privates'."

"I'm sure he didn't." He pointed to the bathroom door. "He's in there now?"

"He and Lewis are bathing together. They have five minutes left." She raised her voice as she said the last three words. "They'd better have their hair washed before they come out as well!"

David heard splashing coming from the bathroom to let him know they'd heard and were obeying. He caught Susan's hand and pulled her down the hall. "I know Albert's giving you fits, but he hasn't obeyed anyone this well since his mother died." He leaned down and kissed her again. "Thank you for getting the boys under control."

She sighed. "The twins are fine. They do what I tell them to do. Lewis is afraid of me, so there's no problem there. Albert, though? He thinks I'm going to give up and let him do what he wants if he fights me long and hard enough. It's not going to happen. If I give in now, I'll never be the supreme ruler of this house, and if I'm not the ruler here, then he will be. And that's *not* happening."

"He comes to me with complaints about you several times per day. He keeps telling me I should have married someone nice who wouldn't have bossed him around all the time."

"And?" She crossed her arms over her chest and glared at him to let him know he'd better take her side.

"I tell him you're his mother and he's going to obey you." How would he dare do anything else? His little wife was fierce, and he wasn't willing to fight her about the boys. He promised her she could do what she wanted as regards their discipline as long as she didn't hit them. She hadn't hit them, but she'd sure made a difference in his household in only two short days.

"Good. The boys don't have it in their heads yet that they need to obey me without question. Well, that's not true. Albert's the only one who is really still giving me any trouble." She sighed. "That boy thinks he can out-stubborn me, but he'll know better soon."

David couldn't help but grin. "I'm sure he will."

"I need to go check on them." She wandered down the hall to outside the bathroom door. "I'm opening this door in one minute. Cover up with towels if you need to!"

David leaned against the wall and watched to see how she handled things. She waited a full minute and then called out, "I'm coming in!"

Albert screamed as she opened the door. "I'm not covered up!"

Susan shrugged. "You had plenty of warning. Cover up next time. Both of you need to get upstairs and get clothes on before lunch. If you can stay clean for the rest of the day, I won't make you bathe before you go to bed tonight. You have to be clean for church tomorrow, though." She held the door wide open so the boys could leave when they were ready.

Albert grabbed a towel and wrapped it around his waist glaring at Susan, before running from the bathroom and up the stairs.

Lewis stood drying off just looking at her. He didn't have a problem with her seeing him naked. "I'll try to stay clean, Ma." He followed his brother up the stairs to dress.

Susan turned to David who was still watching the show. "Well, that was fun. You ready for lunch?"

David walked over to where Susan was standing and pulled her to him hugging her tightly. "You are priceless."

Susan had no idea what he was talking about, but hugged him back. "I'm hungry. What do you think Sadie made for lunch?"

"Let's go find out."

~

THAT NIGHT IN BED, she snuggled against his side. "You know, when Mrs. Hackenshleimer isn't working, you really should try to be at home. The boys need your influence." She'd thought all day about how to have this conversation with him, and had decided to just blurt it out.

"I'm around on Sundays. You only have one day with them alone."

"They need you more than that. You come into the house late in the evenings and are gone Saturdays as well. It's not that I can't handle them. I think I've proven I can. They just need you more than that." She firmly believed that boys needed their father's influence as much as possible, just as girls needed their mother's.

He thought about what she was saying for a moment. The truth was, he could easily spend more time with them. He simply chose not to because they were so difficult. "I'll try."

She nodded, her eyes closing sleepily. "That's all I can ask.

CHAPTER 7

Susan woke early on Sunday morning to make sure she could get the boys ready for church on time. Sadie took Sundays off, which left Susan in charge of seeing to breakfast. She was in the kitchen as soon as the sun was up making French toast and bacon for her new family. She was uncertain how much everyone would eat, so she had a small mountain of food waiting when everyone came down to breakfast.

Susan had Albert pour the milk, and was thrilled to see he followed her instructions immediately. Of course, that was one of the rules she'd made with consequences her first full day there, and he had yet to disobey those rules.

Once breakfast was finished, she sent the older boys upstairs to get dressed for church while she went back into the kitchen. She wanted to go on a picnic after church, so she had fried some chicken while making breakfast. She'd boiled potatoes and eggs for a potato salad, and put it together before going upstairs to get the twins dressed for church.

She noticed the boys had only matching outfits and she wondered if that was a good thing. She decided she'd make them some clothes that were distinct for each of them the first chance she got.

Once the twins were dressed, she sent them to their pa while she got dressed for church herself. She put her dark green dress on, and did her best to imitate the hairstyle Mrs. Duckworth had used for her wedding day. When she looked in the mirror above her dresser, she realized it wasn't perfect, but it was better than her usual style which was just pulling all her hair back into a bun.

She descended the stairs to find all of the boys with her husband waiting in the formal parlor. They were all dressed in their Sunday best and looked good, although Albert's tie was crooked. She walked to him and straightened his tie, but he knocked her hands away.

She raised an eyebrow looking down at him. "I'm trying to help you and you *will* allow me to do it." She spent twice as long as needed straightening his tie, just to show him she could.

Susan walked into the kitchen to get the picnic basket she'd packed along with the quilt she'd put with it. She handed it to David to carry out to the buggy. "We're going on a picnic after church," she announced.

Albert groaned. "I don't want to go on a picnic."

She stared at him. "An eight year old boy who doesn't like picnics? Do you really not want to go on a picnic, or do you not want to go because it was my idea?"

Albert looked down, giving her the answer.

Lewis ran to her and hugged her. "*I* like picnics, Ma."

Susan smiled ruffling his hair. "I'm glad. I like to go on picnics a lot." She looked at David. "Are we all ready?" She knew she'd taken longer than anyone else to get ready for church, but she'd also had the most to do.

"I think so. If no one else needs their tie straightened." David winked at her as he asked the question letting her know he knew she'd spent more time straightening Albert's tie than she really needed to.

She grinned at him and said, "I think the rest of your ties are good." She led the way outside and saw the team had already been hitched to the buggy.

David stowed the basket in the back and then helped her up. He handed her Walter and Thomas. She put Walter in the middle and held Thomas in her lap while the older two boys scrambled into the back.

"Where's a good place for a picnic around here?" she asked David as he pulled out of the driveway and headed south. She'd expected him to head north toward Fort Worth, so she looked at him in surprise. "Where are we going?"

"There's a small country church about a mile down the road, so we go there instead of making the trek into Fort Worth. Most of our neighbors are members there as well, so it's just easier. As for where to go for a picnic, a lot of the members of our church have picnics right there on the lawn after the service. It's a way for people to fellowship without anyone having to go to the trouble of planning a party. Most Sundays there will be a group there unless it's one of the few Sundays where it's too cold or rainy."

"Would you like to join them, or would you rather go somewhere with just the family?" Susan asked. She wasn't sure which she preferred for herself, but she knew it would be good for the boys to have other children to play with.

He shrugged. "If you don't mind, I'd rather go ahead and join the crowd. It'll be nice to introduce you around. It's a small church, and you've met several of the women already, but the sooner you meet the others, the sooner you'll feel a part of the community."

"That sounds good. I assume there will be other children for the boys to play with there." She liked the idea of having a picnic with the church. She did want to meet the other women and make some more friends. Being without her family, no matter how much they annoyed her, in another state made her feel lonely for home.

"Some." He didn't add that several of the families at church didn't let their children play with his boys. Hopefully that ban would be lifted as the boys learned how to behave.

On the way to church, Susan explained to the boys how she wanted them to behave while they were there. "I expect both of you to be on your best behavior. You need to act the way you acted the first night you met me. Before and after the service I want to be able to reach out and touch either one of you. In other words, no running off with friends until I see how you behave. The better you do the more freedom I'll give you next week."

The small country church was similar in looks to the one she'd attended back home. It was a wood building with a tall steeple that had been painted white. She felt right at home as she saw the building and was pleased with it. Someone obviously spent a lot of time seeing to the church property. The lawn was well-manicured, and there were several different flowers thriving along the front of the church. With the drought they were in, someone must be watering them often.

They left the picnic basket in the buggy as they walked into the church. She and David each held the hand of one of the twins, and Susan kept her eyes on the older boys. They listened to what she'd said and stayed right beside her and David the entire time he was introducing her around. The whole congregation only consisted of around thirty people, so there weren't a lot of people she needed to meet. She was pleased with how friendly everyone seemed.

When the preacher got up to start services, she followed David to a pew and they sat with Albert next to her, the twins between them and Lewis on the other side of David. During the first song, she noticed Albert fidgeting and wiggling, and not singing. He acted just as her younger brothers had during church service. She hoped the preacher wasn't long winded, because the boys just didn't have the attention spans for a long service.

The preacher talked about honoring parents that day, and she found herself nudging Albert to pay attention when the preacher talked about obedience. He glared at her, but seemed to at least be listening at some points.

At the end of the service they once again stood to sing, and she leaned over and whispered, "How did you manage to keep these four from running up and down the aisles when it was just you?"

He grinned at her. "It wasn't easy, and I never said they didn't run up and down the aisles during service."

She cringed at the mental image that came to her. She hoped he was kidding, but had a very strong suspicion he wasn't. No wonder the boys had such a bad reputation with the other parents.

After the song, everyone trooped outside. David went to the buggy to get their quilt and picnic basket, and Susan spread the quilt on the ground near the church building. Once everyone was seated on the ground, she fixed plates for them all. David said a prayer for their family and they ate in the sunshine.

After lunch a baseball game was started. Susan watched as the older boys ran off to play. "Are you not going to join in?" she asked David. She noticed that a lot of the other men were playing while the women cheered them on. David seemed as if he would enjoy a game of baseball so she was genuinely surprised when he didn't jump up to join the game.

He shook his head. "I thought I'd spend some time with my wife."

She smiled. The twins were sprawled on the quilt, each of them sleeping. She was surprised they were able to fall asleep in the confusion of the day, but realized they were exhausted from their busy day.

"It seems strange to sit here at a picnic and be the mom instead of just the oldest sister." She'd shared a lot of her mother's duties growing up, and had thought she would feel nothing different when she became a mother to the young boys, but she'd been wrong. The feelings of responsibility were slightly overwhelming for her.

He looked at her. "That's right. You have eleven younger brothers and sisters. What was that like?"

"Chaotic." It was the first word to pop into her head, so of course it was the first word that came out of her mouth. Nothing had ever seemed to go right at home, and she'd always blamed her mother for it. It never occurred to her the sheer number of children could have anything to do with the overwhelming chaos.

"What does that mean?" he asked with one raised eyebrow.

She shrugged. "We never really had any money growing up, so I had to quit school after eighth grade. I watched neighbor kids for extra money, which I gave to my parents to help out with the family expenses. When I wasn't working for someone else, I was watching my younger siblings, or cooking, or cleaning, or sewing. From the time I was six or seven when I wasn't in school I was watching the little ones." She stroked Walter's hair as he slept quietly on the quilt. "My childhood wasn't terrible, don't get me wrong. I just had a lot of responsibilities. My parents were really strict with me and my three siblings who were after me in age. After the four of us, Ma just kind of gave up. She said she was too tired to keep fighting. So the eight youngest kids are monsters."

He smiled at her. "They can't be that bad."

"Our congregation referred to them as 'the demon horde'. The reason I decided to answer your brother's ad was I got home from working all day and found out my younger siblings had tipped over the outhouse while my sister was in it and painted the cow purple. They did all that after having an egg fight in the kitchen and hitting her in the side of the head with an egg." She couldn't help but grin at the memory. "She still had egg shell in her hair."

"Purple?" The laughter was apparent on David's face, but he held it in for her sake.

"Purple. Go ahead and laugh. I know it's funny. I was just so tired of being a surrogate parent to my brothers and sisters I decided to get married." She traced the pattern on the quilt they were sitting on. "I told anyone who would listen that if God ever cursed me with children I'd parent with a very long switch." Her eyes met his as she wondered how he'd react to her mentioning a switch.

He cringed. "You certainly weren't looking for a family like mine then, were you?"

She laughed. "Not at all. The twins are one thing. When you mentioned having two year olds, I knew they were young enough that I could raise them any way I saw fit. The older two are more than I'd bargained for." She watched as Lewis chased the ball across the church lawn. "Of course, Lewis is already straightening up and doing what he's told. Albert and I have a lot more battles of wills ahead of us, I'm afraid."

He took her hand in his. "I'm glad you took a chance on us. I'll help with Albert any way I can."

"This is going to sound silly, but I feel kind of guilty for marrying you when I came out here to marry your brother. It's as if I'm cheating on him somehow." She shrugged to indicate she didn't understand the feelings, but she couldn't deny them.

A look of sadness came over his face at her words. "It doesn't sound silly at all. I know just how you feel. Jesse died a good two weeks before you came here, and I debated with myself every day and finally decided to ask you to marry me the day you arrived. I didn't feel like I should ask you, out of respect for him, but you'd never really met." David stared off into space for a moment. "I'm glad we're married and we really filled a need in each other's lives. You didn't have to go back to 'the demon horde' and I got the wife I needed, but I wish we'd met under any other circumstances."

She nodded. "So do I. What was he like? I mean, I read his letters, but there were only two, and they were bare bones. What was he like as a brother?" She hated how little she knew about the man she had planned to marry. With every day that passed, she thought less about him and more about the man she had married. Was she doing something wrong by not thinking of him more? Was it disloyal to his memory when she really hadn't ever known him?

David smile reminiscently. "There was only three years difference in our ages, and we grew up pretty close. I always wanted to run off and get into trouble, and he was always the voice of reason. He tried to talk me out of so many of the things I did when I was a kid."

"Like what?" She wondered if she really wanted to know what type of trouble he'd gotten into as a child, but she'd learned at their wedding lunch, the boys came by their mischief making tendencies naturally.

He thought hard to come up with a good story. "Well, when I was about thirteen, I had this mean teacher. She was the type who took you back to the cloakroom every day and beat your bottom with a big paddle. I'd been beaten three times that day already, so I wasn't exactly pleased with her. Anyway, at the end of lunch recess, just before she called us back, she always spent a couple of minutes in the outhouse. So, at the beginning of lunch that day, I asked all the other boys for their suspenders and tied them together, and then hid the long rope I'd made out of them in the bushes. When she went into the outhouse, I tied her in there. Charles helped me." He grinned at the memory. "Of course, Jesse was trying to talk me out of it the entire time. I think that's how Miss Schroeder knew it was Charles and me. We got our butts whipped for that one, and we were suspended from school for three weeks. Jesse was suspended too. I thought Ma was going to break her own rule and beat me for sure, but she didn't."

"What did she do?" She wasn't sure if she'd be able to follow his rule and not use a switch on the boys if they did something that bad.

He shrugged. "Told me to go talk to my father."

"What did he do?" She closed her eyes as she waited for the response. *Please tell me his pa at least told him it was a bad thing to do and he should never do anything like that again?*

"He kind of patted me on the head and said, 'Boys will be boys.' Then he let me help him break a new mare he'd just gotten. Loved that horse. She's the dam of most of the horses we have on the ranch today." David grinned reminiscently as he finished the story.

"Sounds to me like you were rewarded for your bad behavior." *No wonder he doesn't have a big problem with most of the things his sons do. His father was even worse.*

"Well, I guess you could look at it that way." David shrugged as if he didn't really care to think about it too much.

"No wonder the boys are so out of control. What kind of parent was Caroline?" *Please tell me she was strict with them, and they've had some discipline in their lives. Otherwise my job is going to be so much harder than it would be.*

He watched Lewis miss the ball as he tried to bat. "Not as strict as you are, but she had the boys under control. Of course, Albert was only six when she died, and Lewis was only four. I don't know how she would have been with the boys at the age they are now."

"You must really miss her." She wondered then if she'd ever live up to his previous wife, but decided not to let it bother her. Caroline had given him four children and years of her life. He'd known her for less than a week.

"Sometimes I miss her. She's been gone for over two years, though, and the mourning period is certainly over." He stretched his legs out in front of him. "She was a good wife to me, and I'm sorry she died, but it's time for me to move on. Even if Jesse hadn't died, I'd have sent off for a mail order bride of my own."

"What exactly happened with Jesse?" She hadn't asked before, because even though she was curious about the exact details, it obviously hurt him to talk about it.

"Jesse came to my house for dinner on the twentieth of July. He was talking about you and how you were going to come out here and marry him. He talked about his plans to buy a ranch in the area. I offered to give him half my ranch, which I've done a dozen times in the past. He refused, saying the spread shouldn't be split, which he always did. Really, the ranch is huge and I wanted to split it with him when Pa died, but he said it needed to be kept together for my boys to inherit." The look of sadness in his eyes made her want to reach out and hug him. "Jesse told me he had to go to The Acre to investigate a murder, and I told him to make sure someone went with him or to go during the day." He took a deep breath. "Jesse had never gone to The Acre at night, but he'd had to go during the day several times to report on different things. He didn't listen to me. Jesse always thought he was invincible. Anyway, he wasn't the object of the gunfire, but he got in the middle of a shoot-out, and a stray bullet pierced his heart. He died right away."

"I'm so sorry." She reached out her hand and squeezed his.

She knew that even though he'd benefited in a way from his brother's death, he would have given anything to still have a brother.

David nodded. "So am I. He was my best friend as well as being my brother. I feel like it's my fault, because he wanted me to go to The Acre with him that night, but another nanny had just quit on me, and I couldn't leave the boys."

"Why did the nanny quit?" She was certain there had to be a reason. The boys probably gave her plenty of reasons to quit.

David grinned sheepishly. "She got tired of the boys putting frogs in her bed."

Susan closed her eyes. "Frogs?" Susan silently vowed to start looking under the covers before she got into bed at night. She wasn't afraid of frogs, but certainly didn't enjoy their slimy feel against her skin.

"Frogs."

"My brothers did that to me until I put a snake in their beds. They never did it again." She shrugged as if she didn't understand why they'd stopped, and gave him her best innocent look.

David laughed. "I know you don't see it, but you are the perfect mother for my boys. You don't take any of their nonsense and you give as good as you get."

"I'm not sure that's such a good thing." Her brothers had loved calling her a tomboy and saying she wasn't "girly" enough to find a husband.

"With my boys it is! You have to be strong enough to fight back, or they'll run all over you."

"Why did I marry you again?"

"You couldn't resist my good looks and charming personality."

She rolled her eyes. "That must be it." Susan moved closer to David and rested her head against his shoulder. She'd gotten up earlier than usual and was getting tired. The heat of Texas was draining for her as well. She'd never felt heat like that. She was thankful they'd found a spot in the shade for their picnic.

"You tired?"

"Exhausted." She was fighting to keep her eyes open.

"Stretch out and go to sleep. There's nothing you need to do right now. It's the perfect opportunity."

She shook her head. "I haven't napped since I was a small child." How could she nap on the church lawn with a baseball game going on just a few feet away?

"Sounds like you've had no time to nap. You do now."

"What about the boys?" Her eyes drifted back to the game both of the older boys were currently engaged in.

"I'm here. I can watch them while you sleep."

"Are you sure?" She'd never been so tempted to take a nap in her life.

"Absolutely." He urged her to put her head in his lap and stretch out. The boys were on either side of her. She was asleep in minutes, and he sat staring down at her, amazed at how young she looked in her sleep. He knew she was only eighteen, but with the boys, she acted as if she'd been in charge of children forever. Of course, with her upbringing she'd been in charge of children since she was a child herself.

He only hoped she'd continue on as she'd started. His boys were a handful, and he was grateful that she was doing so much with them, but more than anything, he was thrilled she was his wife. He'd needed her as much as, if not more than, the boys had. The years since Caroline had died had been extremely lonely. Susan was bringing everything back into focus for him, and he felt like there was now something to wake up for every morning.

That evening the boys all went to bed right after they finished dinner at Susan's insistence. Even Albert only gave a token protest. They were all exhausted after spending a long day outside playing hard.

Susan sat in the family parlor with David reading. It was the first chance she'd had to just sit and relax since she'd been there other than the picnic. She'd done a lot of reading on the train, but she felt as if she spent her whole life looking for ways to sneak off and read on her own.

On her way to bed she stopped to peek in on the boys. She was amazed how young Albert and Lewis looked as they slept. She dropped a kiss on each of their cheeks as she pulled the sheets more snuggly around them.

When she was finished she turned and saw David watching her. She shrugged and walked to the twins' room. "They look like angels when they're asleep."

"If only they acted like them when they were awake," he muttered under his breath.

"They wouldn't be boys if they did." She tucked the sheets around the twins before tiptoeing out of their room.

"Are you glad Mrs. Hackenshleimer's weekend off is over?"

She laughed softly. "I'm ready for her to be back. I can't focus on the older boys as much as I need to when she's not here with the twins." She didn't think she'd need a nanny forever, though. Yes, it was nice, but once the boys were under control, she wouldn't have nearly enough to do.

They went to their room together and she undressed for bed. She was surprised she'd lost her self-consciousness around him so quickly, but she wasn't complaining. Being embarrassed around him every night wasn't something she wanted.

She slipped between the sheets and lay on her side watching him undress. They hadn't made love since their wedding night, because he'd said she needed time to heal. She wondered if he'd try to start something that night. She hadn't seen him naked the one time they'd been together, so she watched with interest. He obviously didn't feel modest as he dropped his pants and underwear to the floor.

When he was standing naked beside the bed, he caught her stare and raised an eyebrow. "Get an eyeful?"

"I did. I didn't see you the other night when we…consummated." Growing up on a farm you'd have thought she'd have seen an adult male nude at least once in her life, but she hadn't. And she certainly hadn't seen an aroused adult male, which was what she was looking at then.

"And?"

She had the grace to blush. "I like what I see," she told him honestly.

He walked around to his side of the bed and pulled her into his arms. "Does this mean you're feeling ready to resume that part of our marriage?"

"I'm not sore anymore if that's what you're asking."

He pressed a kiss to her lips and stroked a hand down her side. "Are you sure?"

She nodded. "I'm positive. I feel good as new."

He slowly moved his hand around to her breast and over her hip. He kept his movements slow and steady to try to ease her into the newness of lovemaking.

After a moment, she pushed against his shoulders until she'd reversed their positions and he was on his back. "You take things so slow!" She kissed him the way he'd taught her, her tongue entering his mouth to tangle with his. Her hands were all over him, stroking him from shoulder to thigh and back again.

She wondered for a moment if he'd mind if she touched him *there*, but decided she didn't care if he minded. She was curious, and she was going to touch him anywhere she wanted. Anything he'd done to her was fair game as far as she was concerned.

Her hand moved down over his belly until she found the part of him she was looking for, wrapping her hand around it, and feeling it grow between her fingers. When he groaned, she jerked her hand away, her eyes going to his face by the light of the full moon shining through their open bedroom window.

He caught her hand and brought it back to him, whispering, "No, don't stop."

She spent a moment stroking him and learning the feel of him, before she rolled to her back again, grasping his shoulder to pull him along with her. "I'm not fragile. I won't break."

He grinned as he followed her down, his hands squeezing her breasts and learning their feel. He was thrilled she was taking such an active part in their lovemaking, and rolled on top of her, spreading her legs with his thigh.

When he entered her this time, she felt only pleasure. None of the pain from the previous time was there. Once he was fully inside her, he paused for a moment, looking down into her eyes in the pale light. "Are you okay?"

"I was until you stopped."

She heard his chuckle as she wrapped her legs around his waist, moving her hips with his to urge him to go faster. She felt the same pressure building inside her as she had on her wedding night, but this time it didn't stop. It kept going until she thought she would break, and then it happened. She felt like her world burst into a million pieces. She bit into his shoulder to keep from shouting and waking the boys.

He groaned as he found his satisfaction and collapsed on top of her. "Are you okay?" he whispered.

She laughed. "I'm more than okay. Can we do that every night?" She was out of breath and eager all at once.

He grinned, brushing a kiss across her neck. "Sounds good to me." He rolled off her and pulled her into his arms.

"If we wake up before the boys, we can do it every morning, too."

"Mmm...going to sleep right now." She felt like she belonged somewhere for the first time since she'd come to Texas. In his arms was where she should be.

CHAPTER 8

*A*fter breakfast the following morning, Susan sat down with just Albert at the table. She'd let him slide on the absolute obedience rule as he'd gotten used to her, and she couldn't let that happen any longer.

Albert sat back in his chair and glared at her, letting her know he didn't appreciate her presence in his house or her insistence they have another "little talk."

Susan cleared her throat before speaking. "I want you to know I've noticed you're not being obedient the first time I tell you to do things. I've been here for long enough now that you know you need to obey. I will start using consequences if you don't obey immediately the first time I tell you to do something. It doesn't matter whether or not you like me. I'm your mother now and I'm here to stay."

"You don't really expect me to do whatever you tell me to do, do you? I mean, you're not my real mom. You're just some girl my dad married."

Susan took a deep breath, mentally counting to ten before responding. "I'm the only mom you've got, and yes, I expect absolute obedience every time I say something. From now on, there will be consequences, and they will be swift. Is that understood?"

"You can't make me do anything I don't want to do. I don't care what you say!" He stood up quickly tipping his chair over in the process.

"Pick your chair up." There was no time like the present to assert her authority and make sure he knew he was going to obey.

"No! You can't make me!" He ran from the room and straight out the front door to the corral where he knew his father was spending the day working with the horses.

Susan left the chair on its side and warned both Sadie and Mrs. Hackenshleimer not to fix it before she followed at a more sedate pace. She'd give Albert time to complain to David about her and tell her what a terrible step-mother she was before she made him do exactly what he'd been told to do.

~

DAVID LOOKED up to see Albert running toward him, his face red with anger and his fists clenched. *He probably had another run-in with Susan. When is he going to understand that she's not going to give up, and he's going to obey her or suffer her consequences?*

"I hate her, Pa. She's so mean to me. Why did you marry her?" Albert had angry tears running down his face and his voice was shaking.

"She's mean to you? What has she done that's mean?" David's voice was calm. He wanted the boy to explain what Susan had done that was so terrible. He was certain she hadn't been mean in any real way, but she did tend to threaten to use a switch on the boys more than he would like.

Albert took a deep breath winded from his run from the

house. "She said I have to do whatever she says whenever she says it. If I don't, she's going to punish me."

"She's your mother now. She has the right to expect obedience from you." David's voice was matter-of-fact, trying to let his son know he would back up Susan if necessary.

"But she doesn't have the right to punish me!"

"What kind of punishment are we talking about? She doesn't have the right to spank you, but she has the right to do anything else necessary to get you to obey." David folded his arms over his chest to see what Albert would say about that.

"She said if I don't obey the first time, I have to do what she told me to do ten times. That's just stupid!"

"Whether you think it's stupid or not, it's your job to do exactly what she says. Did she tell you to do something you didn't do?"

Albert kicked at a clump of dirt on the ground not meeting his father's eyes. "Well, I knocked over my chair by mistake, and she told me to pick it up, but I ran out here to you instead."

David sighed. "Why didn't you just pick it up? Wouldn't that have made more sense? Especially if you knew you'd have to pick it up ten times instead of one if you didn't?"

"I just don't understand why I have to listen to her. She doesn't want me to have any fun anymore."

"She doesn't? Didn't she let you have fun yesterday? Didn't she even encourage you to have fun by fixing a picnic lunch? And she certainly didn't stop you from joining the baseball game."

Albert shrugged. "I guess."

"I think she does want you to have fun. She just wants you to have fun in a way that doesn't hurt others. She wants you to be well-behaved in your fun." He knew at Albert's age, he'd have fought Susan's influence as hard as Albert was, but he needed his son to see she was there to help not hurt.

"I like things the way they were before she came here! Can't you send her back to Massachusetts?"

David grinned despite all his efforts not to. "No, I can't. I married her. You heard the judge. He said, 'Til death do you part.' That means I'll be married to her until one of us dies. And if I kill her, I'll just have to go to prison and never see you again," he added quickly before Albert suggested it.

"Well, I don't want you to go to prison...."

"Good. Because even for you, I wouldn't kill my wife. I happen to like having her around." He saw Susan walking toward them. Squeezing Albert's shoulder, he said, "It's time for you to face the music, son."

Albert looked toward the house. "I guess she's the music."

David chuckled. "She is right now."

"Well, she's definitely not a tune I like."

When Susan reached them, she held her hand out for Albert's. "Are you ready for your punishment?"

Albert looked down at his feet. "I guess so, but do I have to hold your hand on the way back to the house?"

Susan nodded solemnly. "It's part of the punishment. You have to talk to me, too." She knew Albert would rather do anything than hold her hand, so she made a big deal about holding hands with him, swinging their hands back and forth.

David met her eyes and winked at her as he watched them walk back toward the house. He realized a little more every day just how incredible the woman he'd married was.

Susan waited until they were out of earshot of David before saying, "You know you broke the rule we were talking about during our conversation about it." Her voice portrayed just how silly she thought that was.

Albert sighed and kicked at a weed in his path. "I know."

"You know I'm going to punish you for it, right?"

"Yes, ma'am."

"Do you remember the punishment for disobedience?" As if he could forget the punishment when they'd just been talking about it.

"I have to do whatever I was told to do ten times." His shoulders sagged as he said it. "So I get to knock over a chair nine times and pick it up ten?"

Susan shook her head. "No, knocking over the chair is fun, so I get to do that part. You just have to pick it up ten times, and set it right at the table." She did her best not to smile as she told him, because she didn't want him to think she was laughing at his punishment.

"You do know that's stupid, right?"

"I tried to talk your pa into letting me take a switch to your bottom instead, but he said I couldn't. So I have to get creative with 'stupid' punishments." She grinned down at his bowed head. "Would you rather I used a switch?"

"That doesn't sound as stupid as picking up a chair ten times."

She laughed. "It doesn't sound as stupid to me either, but your pa feels differently." She opened the door and waited while he preceded her into the house.

He walked straight to the dining room and picked up the chair he'd knocked over. "One," he said with a groan. She bit her lip to keep from laughing as she knocked it over. He picked it up. "Two."

After he reached "ten" she told him to go into his room for an hour and think about how things could be calmer around the house. After he'd stomped off to his room, she looked up and saw her audience. Sadie, Mrs. Hackenshleimer, Lewis and the twins had all been watching.

She shrugged at the older women. "Well, that was fun."

The sarcasm in her voice told the older women she thought it was anything but fun.

Mrs. Hackenshleimer shook her head. "That boy needs his bottom beaten."

"I don't think we're going to be able to convince David of that," Susan said with a sigh. "Don't worry, though. It's all a game, and it's a game I'm going to win! Children in large families tend to be competitive, and I come from one of the biggest!"

She went back to the family parlor to make clothes that weren't identical for the twins.

~

DURING DINNER THAT EVENING, David was amazed at the difference in his boys. They were all demonstrating the kind of table manners they'd had for Susan's first visit to their house. The twins were even eating with their spoons more and less with their fingers. His eyes met Susan's across the length of the long table.

He gave her a slight smile trying to communicate the difference he saw and how pleased he was about it without bringing it to the attention of the boys. He was truly amazed at how much better all of his boys were behaving after less than a week. He prayed it wasn't just the calm before the storm.

"So what did everyone do today?" he asked.

Albert sighed. "I spent some time in my room thinking about my behavior, and then I found the perfect tree for the tree house you said you'd help me build. When can we get started?"

David was surprised Albert even remembered the promise. It had happened before the twins were born and Albert hadn't mentioned it since. David studied his oldest son. Did he truly understand how difficult life had been for him as a single parent, but now things would be easier because of Susan?

"It's going to be a while. I have three colts I'm training right now, and each one is needed as soon as possible. That means ten hour days six days a week for a while."

Albert pushed his peas around on his plate, obviously annoyed by what his father had said.

Susan had a thoughtful look on her face for a moment before saying, "I could help you, Albert. I helped my younger brothers build a tree house when I was around your age."

Albert stared at her in disbelief. "But you're a girl!"

Susan hid her grin as she shrugged. "I am. I'm also really good with a hammer and saw." She looked at David. "How soon could you get us some lumber?"

"I can request it tomorrow and we could have it by Wednesday. Would it be okay with you if your ma helped with it instead of me?" He held his breath waiting for the answer. This would be such a good way for Susan and Albert to come to terms with one another.

Albert seemed to think about it for a minute. "She wouldn't be allowed in it after she was done, because she's a girl."

Susan shook her head looking very solemn. "Oh, of course not. I would never dream of going in there when it was finished. I'll just help you build it and make sure it's safe." She looked at Lewis who was squirming in his chair with excitement. "You'd help, too, wouldn't you Lewis?"

"Yes!" The single word was shouted in his excitement.

David hid a chuckle as he watched his wife endear his boys to her. Walter looked down at Susan. "Twee house?"

Susan nodded. "Now you boys are too little to climb up in the tree house, but when we're done with the tree house, maybe our building team could build a fort for you."

"Fort?" Thomas asked.

"Do you know what a Fort is Thomas?"

Thomas shook his head, his eyes wide with wonder.

Susan directed her attention to both Thomas and Walter when she told them. "It's a building for just the two of you to play in. No one else would be able to play in your special fort. We could keep blocks and trains in it for you."

"Twains?" Walter asked.

Susan nodded. "Trains. Do you boys want a fort?"

Both Thomas and Walter nodded their heads before returning their attention to their dinner.

Susan met David's eyes. "That's settled then. If you'll get us some wood, the boys and I will start building the tree house on Wednesday."

Albert looked slightly disappointed that he'd be helped by Susan and not David, but he wasn't going to quibble because he wanted to have his tree house as soon as he could. "Will you, Pa?"

David nodded. "I'll order it tomorrow." He could get one of the ranch hands to build it for them, but knew it would be a better experience for the boys, and for Susan, to build it themselves. He hoped this would make Albert feel less animosity toward his new step-mother.

The excitement around the table was palpable. All four boys were glowing at the idea of building places to play, and Susan looked as if she was relieved she'd finally found a way to get through to Albert.

AFTER DINNER, Susan put the little boys to bed, and when she came down the stairs she found David at the table with a pencil and paper and the boys ordering him to draw something. David's eyes met hers. "They want me to help them design the tree house, but I'm not good with drawing. Do you have any idea how to draw a tree house?"

Susan had always been a decent artist. "I can try." She took the paper and pencil from David, and sketched a tree with lots of leaves and several branches that would work for building a tree house. "Is this the kind of tree we have to work with?" She had seen a similar tree not far from the house, but not all the way to the corral and thought that might be the one Albert was talking about.

Albert looked and nodded slowly. "That's the tree. The one that's almost to the corral."

"I know which one you mean. I thought that might be it." She drew a few rectangles spaced about a foot apart along the trunk as footholds for the boys to use as they climbed to the tree house. "We'll pound these in first to make it easier for us to get up there." She drew a large flat base along the top of the lowest branches of the tree. "Now, do you want walls, or should we just build several platforms to give you a several story tree house?"

Albert and Lewis walked into the parlor and Susan and David could hear them whispering, but Susan couldn't make out what they were saying.

"Can we have both?" Albert asked.

Susan shrugged. "Is that okay with you?" she asked David. "You're buying the lumber." Having walls would cost more of course, but she didn't think David would quibble over extra boards.

"I don't see why not. It'll take longer to build, though."

The four of them worked on planning out the tree house until late into the night.

By the time they went to sleep, Susan had a drawing of what the boys wanted for their tree house complete with curtains. "Boy curtains," Lewis insisted. "No flowers. They're too girly!"

"Are you sure you want to do this?" David asked as he climbed into bed and pulled her into his arms. "It's a big project to take on."

Susan smiled. "Some of my best memories of being Albert's age were the hours and hours my brothers and sister and I spent working on the tree house. Of course, we didn't have an adult directing the project and when it was done it looked like it had been built by someone who had over-imbibed in liquor, but we were so proud of it. My younger brothers and sisters still play in it."

David smiled trailing a finger down her bare stomach. "Well, if you want to do it, I certainly won't complain." He kissed her cheek. "I can't believe how much better the boys are already behaving. It's like the difference between night and day."

"I know. I've been happy with them." She traced her finger along his lips. "I'm going to have to hurry if I want to get the twins new outfits done tomorrow."

He frowned. "Why are you making the twins new outfits? I thought they had plenty of clothes."

"Oh, they do. I just think they should be able to dress in non-matching clothes if they'd like. I have younger brothers who are twins, and they hated being forced to match. As soon as they were old enough to speak in complete sentences, they insisted they be allowed to wear things that weren't identical. I think all twins should have a choice." People had often suggested she and Elizabeth should dress alike, and she'd hated the idea so much, she vowed she'd never do that to her children whether she had twins or not.

"They're only two!"

"But they're developing their own individual personali-ties. They don't need to think of themselves as two halves of a whole. They're each people in their own right." Coming from a small family, he wouldn't think about being lumped in with her siblings like she did. People would hear her last name was Miller and step back saying, "One of 'the demon horde.'" The boys didn't need to be lumped together that way.

He shrugged. "I guess."

"If they want to continue to dress alike, they'll have plenty of clothes to be able to do that. I just think they should have a choice." She wanted him to see her point of view, but he seemed to have lost interest.

"Whatever you say," he whispered as his lips went to her neck.

"Mmm…remember you said that."

No words were needed for a long time after that.

CHAPTER 9

Susan spent the following day sewing. She left the boys to Mrs. Hackenshleimer and went to the formal parlor where she knew the boys wouldn't go to play and just sewed as quickly as she could to get the new outfits ready for Walter and Thomas.

Just before noon, Mrs. Hackenshleimer sought her out. "Have you seen Albert and Lewis?" she asked.

Susan's eyes met hers. "I've been here sewing all day. Are they with David?" Both boys enjoyed watching David work with the horses and often spent their mornings sitting atop the corral fence observing the methods he used to break the horses.

"I haven't checked yet, but I don't think so."

Susan bit her lip, wondering if the nanny was just being overprotective or if there was a real problem. "They often spend the entire morning outside, don't they?"

"Yes, they do, but they come into the house by now asking when lunch will be. Those boys are driven by their hunger. They never stay out past eleven because they're so hungry they try to beg for food from Sadie. She's the one who realized they were missing."

Susan set down her sewing and stood. "I'll go check with David." She hurried out the door and to the corral. As she got close, she realized the boys weren't with him. She felt her heart jump into her chest as she broke into a run to talk to him as quickly as she could. "David!"

He turned, smiling at first, but quickly losing the smile as he saw the panicked expression on her face. "What's wrong?"

"Have you seen Albert and Lewis? I thought they were with Mrs. Hackenshleimer this morning, and she thought they were with me. I was sewing, though, and I haven't seen them since breakfast."

David's brows drew together in confusion. "I saw them this morning walking down the road. They said you told them they could walk over to the neighbor's house because they have new kittens."

Susan shook her head. "They didn't mention kittens to me at all. Which way did they go?" She squinted toward the road, hoping she would see them walking back.

"Toward town." He took her by the elbow and led her to the stable. Calling out to one of the men close by, he yelled, "Saddle a horse and hitch up the buggy." He turned to Susan. "Can you drive the buggy?"

"Of course." She'd done enough plowing that driving a buggy was an easy task.

"Okay, I'll ride straight into town and look around for them there. You go to the neighboring ranches and ask around about them. Do you know if anyone has new kittens?"

She shook her head. "If I'd heard about them, I'd have talked to you about getting one for the boys. I know they really want a cat." She was feeling more panicked by the minute. Why would the boys lie about her saying they could do something?

His horse was saddled and he mounted with one lithe motion. "If you find them, come right back here, and I'll do the same. If you don't find them, meet me back here in three hours." He looked down at her, his eyes concerned. "If neither of us have found them in a couple of hours, we'll start a search party."

She swallowed hard and got into the driver's seat of the buggy without waiting for assistance. "Three hours." She drove toward town, but pulled in at the first neighbor's house, while he raced past her into town.

She talked to six neighbors before she gave up to meet David at the ranch. No one had seen the boys. No one knew of any new kittens. The boys had obviously made the story up to do something they knew they weren't supposed to be doing.

As she was pulling into the driveway, she saw David on the horse with both boys riding in front of him. David's face was serious.

She jumped down from the buggy and ran over to the horse waiting until David dismounted and helped the boys down before saying anything. "Where were you two?"

Albert shrugged avoiding her gaze. Lewis kept looking at his feet, obviously afraid to answer.

David put his hand on Albert's shoulder. "Tell her where you were."

Albert pulled away looking up at David. "But she'll punish us, Pa."

David's eyes met Susan's and she realized then whatever they'd done, it was serious.

"Where were you?" She kept her voice calm, but she was screaming inside. She was half afraid of what the answer would be and the other half was furious that they'd frightened her the way they had.

Albert and Lewis exchanged a look before Lewis said, "Well, we wanted to start the tree house sooner, so we went to town to see if we could get some lumber."

Susan put her fists on her hips mentally counting to five before responding. "How were you planning on getting the lumber home once you found it? How were you going to pay for it?"

Albert looked up at her earnestly. "We had a plan. We still have the money Pa gave us to be good the night you came out to see if you wanted to marry him and had dinner with us."

Susan's eyes flew to David and narrowed. He'd bribed his sons to help him deceive her?

"We figured two whole dollars would be enough to buy lumber and have someone deliver it *and* bring us back to the ranch." Lewis continued the story for Albert. "Well, then we got lost, and we ended up in The Acre, and that's where Pa found us, but we didn't mean to be in The Acre, Ma. I swear!"

Susan closed her eyes filled with fury. "The Acre? Your pa found you in The Acre?" Her eyes darted back and forth between the two boys.

Albert hung his head. "Yes, ma'am."

"So let me get this straight. First, of all, you lied to your pa. Then you went into town without permission not letting anyone know where you were really going. And worse than that, you went to The Acre? Where your uncle was killed three weeks ago?" Her eyes met David's. "Am I hearing all this correctly?"

David nodded, his eyes filled with fear. She wasn't sure if he was afraid for what could have happened to the boys or what kind of punishment she had in store for them or for how furious she must be with him for bribing the boys to deceive her in the first place.

"Albert and Lewis, I'd like you to go up to your room and sit on your beds. I don't want you to speak or even look at each other. I'll be up in a few minutes after I've had a chance to talk to your father." Her mind raced about what to do about the boys, but then she shut it down. She'd figure that out after she decided what to do with the man who'd paid his sons to help him deceive her.

Both boys turned and ran toward the house, obviously thankful for what they saw as a reprieve for the punishment they knew was coming.

Susan turned to David. "You bribed your sons to be good so I'd agree to marry you?" She walked toward him utterly furious. She poked him in the middle of the chest and he backed up a step.

"I'm sorry. I know it wasn't the right thing to do, but I saw you and knew you had to be my wife. You're so pretty…"

"That's a bunch of hogwash and you know it! You already told me you were planning to ask me to marry you before you ever saw me. You deliberately deceived me to get me to take on those monsters you call sons." Her voice was low, but filled with fury. She was so angry, she didn't think she'd be able to yell at him until she calmed down.

David continued to back away from her. He'd seen angry women before, but he'd never known one to be as angry as Susan was at that moment. She looked ready to chew him up and spit him out. "I'm sorry."

She closed her eyes fighting her anger. If he'd been one of her brothers, she'd have punched him in the eye without thinking twice about it. She was determined to resolve this without violence, though. "I agree with you. You *are* sorry."

He backed up once more until he felt his horse against his back. "I can't back up anymore, Susan."

"I've never wanted to hit anyone in my life as much as I want to hit you right now." She mentally counted to ten and opened her eyes. "Your boys need a switch taken to them for lying and for going into town without permission. I'm not even going to start on The Acre."

He shook his head. "I just can't agree with beating them. There's got to be another solution."

"Your mother never beat you and look what happened!" She shook her head. "I'm getting off track here. We need to concentrate on the boys. If I can't spank them, you have to stand aside and let me do whatever I want to punish them without hitting." She glared up at him leaving him in no doubt of how angry she still was. "Agreed?"

He nodded. At that point he would have agreed to anything as long as she turned her anger away from him. "What are you thinking?"

"I'm thinking we delay starting the tree house for a day, they get no dessert tonight, and they spend tomorrow cleaning out the stalls."

"No dessert? Make sure Sadie fixes something they don't like."

Her eyes widened. "You're kidding me right? I'm going to go tell Sadie to fix all of their favorite desserts in one night! They will not feel like this punishment is easy!" How could his automatic thought be for making the punishment easier? What was wrong with him?

He nodded, afraid to do anything else at that moment. "Are you sure they should muck out the stalls? That's what the ranch hands are for…."

It was all she could do not to kick the man. What was he thinking? The boys needed a real punishment to keep them from doing the same thing again next week! She took a deep breath and folded her arms across her chest, just then realizing he was cowering against the horse. *Good! He needs to realize I'm angry and I mean business!*

"I will punish them how I see fit, or I will switch them.

Take your pick." She knew her voice sounded gravelly and harsh, but at that moment she didn't care. It was all she could do to speak to him without resorting to violence.

"Do what you want as long as you don't spank them."

"Fine. I will."

She marched off toward the house and went straight to the kitchen, feeling his presence behind her but refusing to acknowledge him.

"Sadie, what are the older boys' favorite desserts?" Her eyes were flashing fire as she asked the housekeeper the question.

Sadie turned with a gleam in her eye knowing very well where this was going after the uproar when the boys disappeared earlier that day. "Albert likes chocolate cake and Lewis prefers blueberry pie."

"Do you have the ingredients to make both for dinner tonight?" The more they loved the dessert the worse the punishment would feel.

Sadie nodded. "I do."

"Please make them."

Sadie grinned. "Are the boys going to bed with no dessert?"

"They are. Among other punishments."

Sadie's eyes met David's over Susan's shoulder. "Not going to argue with her?" The laughter in Sadie's eyes was tangible.

Susan turned and glared at him.

He shook his head quickly. "No, ma'am. I've got more sense than that."

Sadie chuckled. "Looks like you and your boys have met your match, David." She turned back to the stove where she was fixing a thick stew for dinner. "Do either of you need something to eat? You missed lunch…"

David shook his head. "No, the boys and I stopped at a restaurant on our way back from town."

Susan turned and stared at him. "You *what?*"

He shrugged, realizing he'd said the wrong thing. "Well, we were all hungry, and we missed lunch and all…."

Susan couldn't help herself. At that point she pulled her leg back and kicked him in the shin as hard as she possibly could. She could not take another second of his ridiculous parenting methods. "They wander around Hell's Half Acre and you reward them by taking them to a restaurant? What on Earth is *wrong* with you?" She made a shooing motion with her hand. "Get out. Go and play with the horses or do whatever nonsense you do all day. I don't need you here mollycoddling the boys while I'm punishing them. You make me crazy!" She lifted her foot to kick him again as he turned and limped out of the kitchen as fast as he could.

She turned to Sadie. "You've known him his whole life. Was he always *this* stupid?" She wanted to scream. She wanted to take a portrait of the man and hang it on a tree so she could throw axes at it. He should be the one she punished, not the boys!

Sadie was laughing so hard she couldn't respond. She fixed a ham sandwich with leftovers from lunch for Susan and handed it to her.

Susan sat down at the table in the kitchen and ate the sandwich, grumbling under her breath the whole time. "I married a crazy man. He belongs in an asylum. He should not be free to roam around the world."

Sadie watched her while she took out the ingredients she needed to make the desserts the boys wouldn't be allowed to eat.

Finally, Susan finished eating and put her plate in the sink. "Now I have to go deal with his demented offspring. I never thought I'd say this, but I want to go back to Massachusetts and deal with 'the demon horde'. At least there I was allowed to get the switch when the situation warranted it." She grumbled all the way out of the kitchen and up the stairs.

She opened the door to the boys' bedroom and found them facing in opposite directions and not speaking just as she'd told them. *Good. Maybe they learned something from this situation even if their idiot father didn't.*

"First off, I want you to know that you had me frightened half to death this morning. You have been my sons for less than a week, and I thought I'd lost you forever. What on Earth were you thinking going off on your own into Fort Worth that way? You could have been shot or killed!"

Both boys hung their heads. "I'm sorry, Ma," Lewis whispered, obviously contrite.

"We were just trying to help everything get started faster. I'm sorry." Albert looked up at her as he said the last words. "What's our punishment?"

She looked between the two of them utterly fed up with the entire situation. "I wanted to go pick a switch and beat you both with it." She needed them to know that her first inclination was to spank them.

Albert's eyes grew wide. "Teacher does that at school sometimes."

"Good for Teacher!" Susan said emphatically. "Your father doesn't want you spanked, though. I have no idea why, because I can't think of two boys in this world who deserve a spanking more than the two of you do right now." She walked over to look out the window glaring down at David who was back to working with the horses. "You're going to go to bed with no desserts tonight."

Albert let out a huge sigh of relief. He'd obviously expected more.

"*And* you'll spend the rest of the day today, and all day

tomorrow cleaning the stable." She turned back to the boys so she could watch their reaction to her pronouncement.

"But that's what the ranch hands do," Albert said reasonably.

"Yes, it is, and that's too bad. I'd have told them to stop their work for a week if I'd known I'd have to use it as a punishment for you." She thought the boys needed to have real chores anyway. How would they ever learn to be responsible if they were able to play all the time and never work?

Lewis looked up at her, his bottom lip quivering. "Does that mean we don't get to start building the tree house tomorrow?"

"It absolutely means no tree house tomorrow. We'll start Thursday if I get a report that you work hard today *and* tomorrow."

Lewis wiped away a tear that was coursing down his cheek at the idea of putting the tree house off for an extra day. "Yes, Ma."

Albert stood up and grabbed his brother by the arm. "Come on. We need to take our punishments like men." He pulled his brother along behind him.

Susan followed them both down the stairs and out the front door. Instead of going straight to the stable, they first went to their father and said something to him, and then went to the stable. She was certain they'd gone to complain over their punishment, but she was happy to see David backed her up. She had no idea what she was going to do with David. *Is he too old to take a switch to?*

DAVID STOOD STARING at the boys after they left him to go clean out the stalls. When they'd come toward him, he was sure they were coming to complain about their punishment, and he was going to find a way to sneak around Susan and go easier on them. Instead, their purpose in coming to see him was apologizing for causing him worry. He couldn't believe it. Why hadn't they asked him to not have to muck out the stalls?

When he went into the house for dinner, he found Susan in the formal parlor finishing up some sewing for the twins. "Those look nice," he commented.

She grunted but didn't say anything, so he assumed she was still angry with him for several different reasons. He sighed and went upstairs to change for dinner. He didn't want to stay in a room with a wife who was obviously furious with him, for good reason, he had to admit. He'd really messed things up, and wondered what he'd have to do to get her to forgive him.

When he went down the stairs after changing, he saw Albert and Lewis with Susan. She'd finished her sewing and had laid it aside, and the boys were apologizing to her. He couldn't believe his ears. Had she told them they had to apologize?

Susan hugged both boys to her. "Thank you for saying you're sorry to me. I want you to know that I understand you just want to have fun. I want you to have fun. But you have to do it in a way that's safe for you and for other people. Running around town without anyone knowing where you are is not safe. Anything could have happened to you."

Albert pulled away. "We know you're just trying to keep us safe, Ma. Thanks for caring about us."

David was shocked. Surely now she'd tell the boys they could have their desserts back and they didn't have to spend the next day mucking the stalls. He waited for a minute for her to say so, but she didn't.

He stepped into the parlor. "You boys have obviously learned your lesson. I think you can have your desserts tonight, and you don't have to finish up the horse stalls tomorrow."

Albert looked surprised and turned to Susan. "Is that true, Ma?"

Susan shook her head. "I can tell you've learned your lesson, but you need to understand there are consequences for everything you do. You'll finish up your punishment, and then everything will be back to normal again." She ruffled both boys' hair. "Go wash up and change your clothes for dinner."

As soon as the boys were out of the room, she stood up glaring at David.

"They've learned their lesson. Why can't you just end the punishment now?" David was surprised she was clinging to a punishment for a lesson they'd obviously already learned.

"Because if I stop their punishment every time they come to me and apologize and hug me, they'll do that as soon as they've done something wrong and realize they can get away with anything. They need structure in their lives and cutting off their punishment is *not* structure." She took a deep breath, obviously searching for self-control. "I would appreciate it if you would consult me before rescinding any punishment I give in the future. They need to see us as unified when it comes to discipline. If I decide to stay here, I need you to back me up every step of the way."

His eyes widened in shock. "What do you mean if you decide to stay?" She wasn't seriously thinking about leaving him was she? They hadn't even been married for a week!

"Just that. I found out today my husband deliberately deceived me and it's obvious he's trying to undermine me with our boys. I won't stay in a marriage where that contin-ues." She walked past him into the dining room where Sadie was serving the stew she'd made with some homemade biscuits. She took her seat at the foot of the table while Mrs. Hackenshleimer brought the twins to their high chairs.

"Thanks for all your help today, Mrs. Hackenshleimer."

The nanny nodded, and started toward the kitchen. "Is that all for the night?"

"Yes, I'll put them to bed after dinner."

David watched the whole exchange still feeling shocked to his core. Was his wife going to leave him? Christian wives didn't just leave their husbands over something little. What was she thinking?

He watched as Albert and Lewis took their seats before taking his own. He calmly prayed over the meal and they all ate. Albert and Lewis seemed happier than they'd been in a long time. How was that possible? They were being forced to carry out a severe punishment. How could they be happy?

David didn't understand anything that was going on around him. Whatever was happening with his boys was beyond his understanding. Did they *want* to be disciplined? Caroline had told him more than once that children liked structure, but did that mean they were happier when they were punished? It didn't make sense at all.

When Sadie brought out their favorite desserts, both boys looked sad, but they never reached for a piece knowing they wouldn't get them. Neither boy complained. David wanted to give them each a piece because of their sad looks, but he didn't want to lose his wife, and he was afraid he'd already done that. He sighed. Why did the boys seem to think her decisions were good while they ignored his?

Susan put Thomas and Walter to bed immediately after dinner. When she came down the stairs afterward, she told the older boys to take baths and wash their hair. "Do you need me to help you with your hair Lewis?"

"I'll help him, Ma. I don't mind." Albert smiled at Susan as if she'd granted him a favor that day instead of depriving him of one of his favorite things.

Susan nodded at Albert. "That would be good. Thanks for helping your brother." She calmly walked into the family parlor as if Albert offered to help do things for his younger brothers every day and plucked a book off the shelf. She was sitting quietly reading when David walked into the room, still flabbergasted about what he'd seen.

He sat next to her on the couch, and she stood and moved to the overstuffed chair in the corner of the room. "May I ask you something?" David asked cautiously. Susan gave a quick nod, but didn't look up from her book. "Why are the boys acting as if you've given them some sort of gift when all you did was punish them today?"

She put her open book against her belly, and her eyes met his for the first time since their confrontation before dinner. He could see the anger still seething in her green eyes, and hoped she got over her mad before bed that night. He was half afraid he'd wake up with a knife at his throat.

"Children *like* structure. They like knowing what the rules are and what the consequences will be when they break the rules. It makes them feel safe to know there are rules in place, especially when they understand why the rules are there. After they've broken a rule, they feel lost until someone punishes them, and then they feel better about it again."

"You really believe that, don't you?"

"With everything inside me. I'm not just trying to be mean to the boys. I want them to be well-behaved, yes, but I also know they'll be happier if they have the structure I'm creating. Sure, they enjoy running around like crazed heathen children, but they prefer to follow a structure."

David sat back and thought about what she'd said. The boys seemed, by their behavior, to be telling him she was right. Even Albert was becoming helpful and obedient. "Are you really thinking about leaving me?" He regretted the question as soon as he'd asked it. He didn't want her to realize just how her threat had made him feel. He couldn't go back to the way things had been before they'd married. He was relying on her too much already, and they'd only been married a few days.

She sighed. "I promised both my mother and the woman who runs the mail order bride agency that sent me here that I wouldn't put up with being married to a man who mistreated me. I think they meant not to put up with a man who beat me, but I think bribing your boys to deceive me and contradicting my punishments is just as bad. I can't stay somewhere where that kind of treatment is a way of life. I won't. I respect myself too much for that." Her eyes met his again, the anger gone but the serious look told him she wasn't joking about leaving. "I don't want to leave. Now that the boys are mostly under control, it's pleasant here. I enjoy being married to you. I just can't allow any man to lie to me and get away with it."

David groaned. "I'm sorry. I shouldn't have done that. I had no idea how strongly you felt about poorly behaved children, but that's no excuse. I just wanted to be married again and have help with them, but I shouldn't have done that to you or any other woman. Will you forgive me?" His eyes were intense as they looked into hers, trying to determine just how angry she was.

She nodded slowly. "We'll start fresh, but now you know the kind of things I absolutely cannot tolerate."

"I do. Things will be better around here. I promise."

SUSAN LEFT explicit instructions with Sam, who was in

charge of the stables, before she left for coffee with Beverly and Wilma the following afternoon. The boys needed to work continuously and not take more than one fifteen minute break. Sam just nodded at her, obviously afraid to argue with her. He hitched the team to the buggy and watched as she drove off for coffee and cookies with her new friends.

David had given her instructions in how to get to the neighbor's house, and she saw that Wilma was just getting out of her own buggy as she pulled up. "Wilma!" Susan called waving to her friend.

Wilma waited for Susan with a grin on her face. "I'm so glad you and Beverly invited me today," Wilma said shyly.

Susan linked her arm through the other woman's and led her to the door. "Why's that?"

Wilma shrugged. "I've kind of kept to myself over the years, and the friends I made in school all moved on without me. Now that I'm married, I'd like to be able to do things with other ladies, but I'm just not sure how to go about it."

Susan smiled at her. "Well, you've gotten started now. Next Wednesday we'll meet at my house at the same time, and maybe the following week the three of us can meet at your house. I'm sure we'll all be great friends in no time." She truly enjoyed being around Wilma. Wilma seemed extremely shy, and Susan knew that shy women did better when they had outgoing friends. Susan didn't have a shy bone in her body.

Beverly opened the door before they had a chance to knock. "Come in! I have the coffee and cookies all ready."

Susan glanced around the house as she went in. It was as nicely furnished as the Dailey home, and she immediately wondered if Beverly had an indoor outhouse as well. She followed the other woman into the parlor and sat down on the couch. "Where are your girls?" Susan asked. She'd met the three girls at church on Sunday and had expected to see them again that day.

Beverly smiled. "I sent them into town to stay with their grandmother. She's been itching to have them for a day, and I thought we'd have more fun without them here."

Susan relaxed against the back of the couch. "Good. I could use an afternoon with no children." She rolled her head on her neck, feeling extremely comfortable with both of her new friends.

Beverly looked over at her. "You getting anywhere with those hellions?"

Susan nodded. "I really think I am. Of course, Albert and Lewis went to Fort Worth yesterday and got lost. They ended up in The Acre." She said the words casually knowing they'd have more impact that way.

Wilma gasped. "They're okay?"

"We realized they were missing and went looking for them. I think I went to every ranch north of ours." She looked at Wilma. "You must be south of us as well."

"We share a border with Beverly on her south side."

"Well, the two of them are at home mucking out the horse stalls. I wish David would let me spank them, but he's adamant." She stretched her arms above her head. "It's hard being married to someone who feels as differently about discipline as David and I do." She shook her head as she thought about the arguments she'd had with David in the past week regarding discipline.

Beverly nodded. "I'm glad Charles and I don't have that problem. Of course, our girls are very well behaved."

Susan nodded. "Compared to my boys most children are. They're improving, though. I just have to keep telling myself that."

"So how are you enjoying married life other than the boys?" Wilma asked.

"Other than the boys and fighting over the boys, it's good. We do fight over them a lot more often than I like." Susan shrugged. "I do enjoy being married, though. David is a good husband for the most part."

Beverly leaned forward. "Do I sense trouble in paradise?"

"A little." She wondered if it would be right to tell them what had happened, but decided she needed advice and the two of them were there. It would take a month to get a letter from back home if she wrote asking someone there for the advice she needed. "I found out yesterday he paid the boys to be good the night I met them. He knew I wouldn't marry him if I saw how the boys really acted."

Beverly's eyes widened and then her lips quirked. "I know it was wrong, and deceptive, but it's funny."

Susan shook her head. "The boys just casually mentioned the dollars he'd given them to be good so I'd marry him. I was so furious with him I threatened to leave him."

Wilma hid her smile behind her hand. "You haven't even been married for a week. You can't leave him."

"Oh, I could! But I won't. He does know now that I won't put up with that kind of nonsense." She picked up a sugar cookie and took a bite. "Why couldn't he have simply said, 'My boys are hellions, but I think you could get them to act right in no time?'"

Beverly gave Susan a knowing look. "Would you have married him if he had?"

Susan shook her head with a laugh. "Absolutely not."

"That's why he didn't say it then," Beverly said.

Wilma smiled at Susan. "I can't help but remember how bad David, Charles and Jesse were in school. Every time I turned around they were getting in trouble for something."

Beverly looked at Wilma. "What about Ned? Wasn't he part of it?"

Wilma blushed. "Ned was too busy making eyes at me to

get into trouble. We spent all of our recesses together even back then."

Susan tilted her head to the side as she studied Wilma. "Why did he join the army then? Why didn't he just stay here and marry you right after school?"

Wilma looked down at her hands. "There was another boy who Ned thought I loved. We were just friends, and I was helping him to court another girl, but Ned saw us and thought there was more between us, so he joined the army. By the time he knew the truth, it was too late. He asked my pa if he could court me as soon as he came back, though." Wilma took a sip of her coffee. "I think we're closer because of the years apart. I think it taught us just how much we cared for one another. We did write to one another as often as possible, but it just wasn't the same as being together."

Susan sighed. "I love good love stories like that."

They spent the rest of the afternoon laughing and joking about the antics the men had pulled when they were boys and the problems Susan's boys were causing. Susan looked at Beverly just before she left. "One day, one of my boys is going to marry one of your girls and there's nothing you can do about it."

Beverly leaned back and groaned. "That's the last thing I need!"

Wilma laughed. "I hope it happens."

Beverly glared at Wilma. "Then I hope you have a girl for one of her twins to marry."

Wilma smiled at Susan. "I wouldn't mind being related to Susan through marriage."

They all laughed, and agreed to meet at Susan's house the following week at the same time. Susan was happy to have made two such good friends so soon after she arrived. She and Wilma walked out to their buggies together. "I'll see you Sunday," she called as she drove north toward her home.

Wilma waved at her, looking much happier than she had when Susan had met her at their wedding. Susan was glad she'd reached out to the shy woman, because she firmly believed a good friend could make all the difference in the world.

CHAPTER 10

*T*hings around the ranch became easier to deal with as the time passed. She helped the boys build their tree house, and then the three of them built a fort for the two younger boys. She made curtains and bought small rugs for the floors of the boys' structures. Once the fort was built, it seemed as if she never saw Albert or Lewis anymore, because they spent their time in the tree house, planning their takeover of Texas and then the world, although they did still hold the belief that Texas *was* the world.

The twins enjoyed their fort, but didn't spend nearly as much time in it as the older boys spent in the tree house, because either Susan or Mrs. Hackenshleimer had to be in the fort with them, and they'd picked up the idea of "no girls allowed" from their older brothers. They thought the women should stand outside the fort and watch them through the window, and neither of the women was willing to stand in the hot Texas sun to do that for long.

David and Susan made peace with one another, and he deferred to her judgment when it came to disciplining the boys. She was still wary of him, and unsure of whether he was going to give her the full authority she needed to keep the boys in line, but she was certainly enjoying their marriage. Yes, the days were long, but the nights were wonderful. She loved being married to David. She often wondered if she'd have gotten bored being married to Jesse.

Susan expected the temperature to cool off once September hit and the older boys started school, but the hot Texas sun just kept beating down on them. One Tuesday afternoon, toward the end of September, she was working on sewing some winter clothes for the twins. They did prefer to dress in different colors instead of always dressing alike, so she was trying to give them a variety of clothes to choose from. Baxter, their new kitten was curled up on the couch next to her, hiding from the twins to catch a nap.

Walter walked into the family parlor where she was doing her sewing and squatted down to play with his blocks. After a moment, she could smell his diaper, and looking up, she saw brown lines dripping down his legs. She made a face and set her sewing down, scooping him up and holding him at arms' length to take him to the bathtub, hoping she wouldn't get anything on her.

As soon as she started the water in the bathtub, Mrs. Hackenshleimer came up behind her with Thomas on her hip. "Do you want me to do that?"

Susan shook her head. "I can do it. Would you mind getting his dirty clothes to Sadie right away, though? And getting me some clean clothes for him?" Susan knelt beside the tub with Walter standing naked in his bath giggling as she used a glass to dump water over his back and legs.

Mrs. Hackenshleimer put Thomas down and told him to go play with the blocks in the family parlor before she left to do what Susan had asked. When she returned, Walter was sitting in the bathtub, splashing happily. He rarely got to take a bath without his brother, so Susan was letting him enjoy himself.

After Mrs. Hackenshleimer set Walter's clean diaper and fresh clothes on the floor beside Susan, she said, "We need to talk about potty training these two. They're plenty old enough to be using the toilet like the rest of the family."

Susan nodded. "I totally agree. I think I'll have the older boys take them outside and show them how to 'water the flowers' they see. Albert and Lewis won't like it, but they'll do it."

Mrs. Hackenshleimer smiled as she leaned against the door jam. "The difference you've made in those two older boys is simply amazing. They were hellions when I first arrived. They tried to hide it, because they were afraid of me, but I could see it. That first night you came, I wanted to warn you to run as fast as you could in the other direction, but I can see now, you're just what this family needed."

Susan was surprised by the compliment from the older woman. Mrs. Hackenshleimer was always so serious and focused on her job Susan hadn't realized she paid that much attention to what was going on in the family other than the twins. "Thank you. It's nice to hear someone has noticed."

"Everyone has noticed. You have worked wonders with the boys, and we're all happier for it." She glanced around and tilted her head to the side as if she was listening for a moment. "I don't hear Thomas."

Susan glanced at her. "I'm sure he's just playing with the blocks like you suggested."

Mrs. Hackenshleimer nodded. "Excuse me for a moment while I go check." She was back a few moments later. "He's not there. Why do we keep losing the boys?"

Susan jumped up, knowing she could cover more ground looking for the child than Mrs. Hackenshleimer could. "You finish his bath. I'll go look for Thomas." She ran through the house calling the boy's name, but there was no response.

She rushed into the kitchen her eyes frightened. "Have you seen Thomas?"

Sadie turned away from the chicken she was frying for dinner. "No, is he missing?"

"Yes, we told him to play with the blocks while we were washing Walter. He's not anywhere in the house I can see." She hurried toward the door to the dining room. "I'm going to go get David to help me look for him."

She ran out of the house, calling Thomas's name. She checked in the fort, but he wasn't there. She couldn't see him anywhere. Running toward the corral still calling his name, she saw David turn to her with a concerned look. "Thomas is missing. We were giving Walter a bath and he was playing with blocks, and then suddenly he was gone."

David noted the panicked look on his wife's face and pulled her into his arms. "We'll find him." He called out to the nearest ranch hand that Thomas was missing, and the man ran to tell the others. "How long has he been missing?"

Susan shook her head. "Not more than twenty minutes. I'm so sorry, David." Tears were coursing down her face. "I can't believe I've lost him." She should have paid more attention to Thomas than she had. She could have handled getting Walter's dirty clothes to Sadie and taken Walter upstairs naked. She'd done it before. Why had she asked Mrs. Hackenshleimer to put Thomas down?

David took her hand and walked with her. "Where's the kitten?"

"I'm not sure. He was sleeping beside me on the sofa while I was sewing, but then Walter made a huge mess, leaking out of his diaper, and needed to be bathed right away. I didn't notice him again after that. He may still be sleeping in the family parlor."

"You run and check, while I search all the outbuildings. He couldn't have gone far. His legs aren't long enough to cover much distance." David turned toward the pigpen first. He knew how much the twins enjoyed chasing the pigs now that Albert had taught them that game.

Susan ran out of the house a few minutes later. "Baxter is missing too."

David nodded. "I have a feeling we'll find the two of them together."

They searched the stable, but he wasn't there. Sam said he hadn't seen any of the boys that day. Susan was terrified. The ranch was huge and anything could happen to Thomas on it. He was so small. What if he wandered into the corral and got kicked by one of the horses?

Finally, they checked the barn, and there was Thomas, sitting in the corner playing with Baxter. Susan ran to him, picked him up and hugged him to her. Tears were coursing down her face and she didn't care. She'd been so worried she'd lost him.

Thomas pulled away after a moment. "Mama cry?" He poked one of the tears with his finger.

Susan gave a half laugh. "I thought we lost you."

"I play with kitty." His face made it clear he thought she was crazy to be so worried when he was just playing with the animal.

She put Thomas back down. "You can play with kitty." She turned to David and saw him watching with a relieved smile. She walked into his arms and held him tightly. "I thought we'd lost him. I'll never let him out of my sight again." She knew she was being melodramatic even as she said it, but she couldn't stop the words. How could she live with herself if something happened to one of them?

David laughed. "Of course, you will. He's fine."

Susan shook her head. "I don't know what I'd do if we lost

one of our boys." Her voice was still shaking as she thought about what could have happened.

David smiled, stroking her hair. "Our boys?"

She nodded. "Of course, they're our boys."

"Does that mean you're glad you married me?"

She laughed softly. "Of course, I'm glad I married you. I have a man I couldn't live without, and four boys I love with all my heart." How could he not know that after six weeks of marriage? Didn't she show him every day how much she loved them all?

David gave her a serious look. "Is it only the boys you love?"

She smiled, stroking his cheek. "Of course, it's not. I love you more than I ever dreamed I'd love anyone. I don't think I knew how much I loved all of you until Thomas went missing, though. It's amazing how losing a child puts everything in perspective." She looked over at Thomas looking so content as he played with the kitten giggling.

"I'm so glad," he whispered, kissing the top of her head. "I think I fell in love with you when you got so mad at me on our wedding day."

Susan laughed. "So what you're saying is what you love most about me is my horrible temper?" She thought about how she'd poked him in the chest and told him there was no way she'd share a bed with him.

"I wouldn't go that far."

Susan took Thomas's hand before putting her arm around David's waist and walking toward the house. "Well, if it's when you knew you loved me…." She couldn't believe she felt good enough to tease him so soon after the crisis with Thomas. It was amazing what the words, "I love you" could do.

"I was just so glad to see you had spirit. So many women

let men run all over them, and I'm so proud that you don't do that."

She realized the older boys had made it home from school as she walked toward the house.

Albert looked at her with a shocked look. "You okay, Ma? You look like you've been crying. You never cry."

Susan laughed self-consciously. "Thomas wandered off and we couldn't find him. It really scared me." She knew Albert would worry if he didn't know exactly what had happened.

Albert stared at her for a moment. "Is that how you felt when Lewis and I were missing that day?"

"It is absolutely how I felt. I don't want anything to happen to any of you boys." She shook her head thinking back to her dread from that day as well. She'd never lost her siblings at home, but they didn't tend to wander, and when they did, they left a trail of destruction that was easy to follow.

"Does that mean you're going to stay?"

Susan's eyes widened in surprise. "Of course I'm going to stay. Why would you think I wouldn't?" Susan had no idea he was worried about her leaving them. Had he heard what she'd told David the day he and Lewis had gotten lost in The Acre?

He shrugged and kicked a pebble. David took Thomas's hand and led him into the house. "Well, my real ma left. And all the nannies left."

Susan put her arm around Albert's shoulders and led him to the porch swing where they both sat. "Your real ma left because she died. She didn't want to leave you. And the nannies left because you and your brother did mean things to them. Why did you do that?" She knew she should be focused on his worries of her leaving, but since he was opening up to her, she really wanted to know their reasoning for being so mean to the different nannies.

Albert shrugged. "We didn't really want them here. Most of them just wanted to marry Pa. They didn't care about us."

"I do." Susan was sure he already knew it, but she told him anyway.

"I know, Ma." Albert rested his head on her shoulder. "I'm glad you were the one who didn't leave."

"I'm not going anywhere." She was happy to be able to reassure him of that fact. She couldn't imagine life without her husband and boys. "I love you and your brothers."

"I love you, too, Ma."

They sat together silently for a few minutes each of them happy the other was there. Finally, Susan asked, "Are you hungry? Sadie was making fried chicken a while ago. I bet it's done." She knew fried chicken was his favorite meal.

Albert stood up and offered her his hand to help her.

"Thank you, sir." She accepted his help gracefully and they went into the house together.

Sadie was just putting dinner on the table. Mrs. Hackenshleimer stood beside the table wringing her hands together. "I'm so sorry I lost him. I'll go pack my bags."

Susan stared at her in disbelief. "You can't abandon me now!" She didn't want to think about doing it all alone without the older woman's help.

Mrs. Hackenshleimer looked at Susan in surprise. "You mean I'm not fired?"

Susan shook her head. "Of course not! I need you!" She walked over and hugged the older woman. "You were the one who realized he was missing which is why we found him so quickly. I don't know how long he would have been gone if you hadn't said something when you did."

"But I was the one who lost him in the first place!"

"We lost him together. We were both focused on other

things and weren't paying enough attention." She wasn't going to let the nanny take the full blame for something she'd done wrong as well.

Mrs. Hackenshleimer nodded slowly. "You still want me to stay?"

"Absolutely! Who else is going to help me potty train the twins?" Susan grinned at the nanny. "You're done for the night, though. Go get your dinner."

"Thank you."

Susan took her seat at the foot of the table. The boys sat in the exact same places they'd been in the first time she'd eaten with them, and she realized the meal was the same, too. So much had happened in the time she'd been in Texas, and she was thankful she had her family. She remembered then she was supposed to write Harriett a few weeks after the wedding and let her know everything was all right. She made a mental note to write to her first thing in the morning so she wouldn't forget.

They all joined hands and David prayed over the food, thanking God that Susan was in their lives and that they'd found Thomas. Thomas still had no idea he'd caused such an uproar, but he liked hearing his name in the prayer.

Susan turned to Lewis. "So how was school today?" She'd found that asking Lewis before she asked Albert was always a good thing. Lewis tended to not only tell her everything Albert had done wrong during the day, but he happily told on himself as well.

"Albert was making faces at Ruby again. He had to stand in the corner."

Susan looked at Albert. "Who's Ruby?" Was there a girl in the boy's future? Wasn't Ruby one of Beverly's daughters?

Albert blushed. "Just a girl."

"Is she pretty?" Susan wiggled her eyebrows as she asked the question, knowing her teasing would embarrass him.

He shrugged.

"What's her last name?" She wasn't going to give up until she knew everything there was to know about the little girl he made faces at during school. Wilma had said that was how her relationship with Ned had started.

"Smith."

Susan looked at David. "Is Ruby Charles and Beverly's daughter?" She tried to keep the absolute glee from her voice as she asked the question. Beverly would be beside herself is something happened between Albert and her precious little Ruby.

"Yes, she's their oldest. Why?"

Susan's smile lit up her entire face. She couldn't wait until Wednesday so she could torment her friend over the fact that Albert thought her daughter was pretty. "No reason." The smile didn't leave her face as she continued her meal, though. She and Wilma were going to have a lot of fun teasing Beverly.

∼

IN BED THAT NIGHT, David asked Susan why she'd been so excited to know Ruby was Beverly's daughter.

Susan laughed. "Beverly's convinced her perfect girls won't marry any of our hellions, and Albert thinks ruby is pretty. She's going to have a fit when I tell her about it tomorrow."

David grinned. "Charles won't be happy either. Let's have them over for dinner so we can watch them squirm when Albert looks at their girl."

"Yes, let's!"

She sounded so excited at the prospect of watching their friends discomfort he couldn't help but laugh. "You have an evil streak, wife."

"And you like it, husband."

"Why yes. Yes, I do." He pulled her to him more tightly, loving even her mean streak. He would never have guessed when she stepped off the train just how well she fit in with his family.

"It's why you love me."

He chuckled. "It's only one of the many reasons I love you."

"Just so there's one." She snuggled into his side and rested her head on his shoulder. "I made the right decision marrying you."

He hugged her closer. "I know you made the right decision for me and my boys." He'd known that since the first week they'd married. How had he been so fortunate?

"Our boys."

EPILOGUE

*J*anuary 5th, 1885

Dear Harriett,

I was very happy to receive your letter yesterday. Things are still going very well for me here. I know I came to you determined that I didn't want to marry a man who had children, but I'm so glad things worked out the way they did.

My boys make me smile every day. I can't imagine what life would be like without them. Thomas and Walter are potty trained now. I can't believe they'll be three next month! Albert is still sweet on our neighbor's daughter, little Ruby Smith. I tease her mother constantly about Albert being her future son-in-law. Lewis is determined he's going to join the army to fight Indians as soon as he finishes school, and I pray every day he outgrows that notion.

My life is so very different than what I pictured it would be when I left Beckham, but it's no less wonderful than I'd imagined. Thank you so much for helping me.

I wish you every happiness in your future. If you ever need something from me, please don't hesitate to contact me. I think of you as one of my very dearest friends and will always be grateful for the life I have thanks to your service. I look forward to hearing from you soon.

Yours,
    Susan

SUSAN FOLDED the letter to get it ready to post. She still wondered what had happened to leave Harriett a widow at such a young age. And why did she limp? She knew they were questions she'd never be able to ask. She did hope her friend found happiness, though. It was sad to see such a pretty woman devote her life to others' happiness and never find a true love of her own. Someday, she hoped to receive a letter telling her Harriett had found love.

EXCERPT: MAIL ORDER MIX UP

June, 1885 Beckham, Massachusetts

Ellen Bronson washed the last dish straining her mind to come up with a way to get money to come up with more food. She and her younger sister, Malinda, were down to their last pot of beans. There was just enough corn meal for one more pan of corn bread, and then they had nothing.

When their father had died just two weeks before, they'd been convinced that they'd find where he'd hidden the money he'd saved, but the more they searched the more despondent they became. They'd finally come to the conclusion that there was no money to be found. They'd always lived a good life, albeit a simple one living on the outskirts of Beckham, Massachusetts on a small farm. The two sisters had continued to milk the cows that kept their dairy farm afloat, but the dairy told them they'd already paid their father in advance for the entire month. It was the fifteenth, and they had no money, and as far as Ellen could see, no way to get more.

Malinda put away the bowl and put it in the cupboard. "What are we going to do?"

Ellen shook her head despondently. "I have no idea. Dad always kept up with the money. He never even discussed it with us, always just saying it wasn't something we should be worried about."

The two sisters were both slim with dark hair. Ellen's hair was a medium brown, while Malinda's was so dark it was almost black. Ellen had grey eyes, exactly the color of a dark cloud just before a storm. Malinda's eyes were a brown that always seemed to be filled with laughter. The two sisters were only eleven months apart, with Ellen being the elder.

Because they had lost their mother at a young age, they had grown closer than most sisters and tended to do most things together. Ellen was the natural leader between them, not only because she was slightly older, but because she actually enjoyed doing the work around the farm. Malinda would rather curl up with a good book than clean the house, but she always helped when asked. Together they'd worked to keep the farm going since their father had died. Just a couple more weeks and they would have some money again, and be able to buy more food. They could make it. They just had to tighten their belts a bit.

"I know. But now I'm getting worried. Should we go see the man at the bank and see if he had some money there for us?" Malinda asked.

"He always said the safest place to keep your money was in your own house. He didn't trust bankers. There's no way he'd have had a bank account and not told us about it."

Malinda leaned against the cupboard drying her hands on her apron. "I know. I just don't know what else to think."

"I don't either." Ellen sighed heavily, looking around the kitchen. "I guess we need to find something to sell. I've looked for a job in town, but it takes both of us to get all the milking done. We only need to be able to find enough money for food for the next two weeks, and then we'll get paid again." Ellen rested her hand against her stomach, which was still hungry despite just having eaten. There was so little food left, she tended to take small portions for herself claiming to not be hungry, so Malinda wouldn't have to go without.

Malinda looked out the open window with the blue checked curtains that fluttered in the June breeze. "There's someone here in a fancy black carriage!"

Both sisters removed their aprons and stepped outside. Ellen brushed her hair away from her face and looked up at the tall middle-aged man in front of her. His salt and pepper hair was groomed immaculately. "May I help you?" she asked.

"Are you Ellen and Malinda Bronson?"

Both girls nodded. "Yes, sir," Malinda answered.

"I'm Jacob Baxter." He brushed some dust off of his immaculate black suit as if he were too good to even be standing on a farm.

They stared at him blankly for a moment. He seemed to think they'd know who he was so Ellen said, "I'm sorry. I don't know who you are." She did know he wasn't someone she liked, though. He obviously thought he was much better than she and her sister.

"I'm the manager of the bank in Beckham. Your father never mentioned me?"

The sisters exchanged a quick look. "Never," Ellen responded. *What is he doing here? And how did he know my father? He surely would have mentioned if he'd had business with the bank in town.*

"I was afraid of that. Your father took out a loan a few months back to buy some more cattle. Did he mention that to you?"

"No, sir." Ellen looked at the man skeptically. "Do you have proof?"

He pulled a document out of the briefcase on the front seat of the carriage. "Everything is right here. You'll see he signed it at the bottom."

Ellen skimmed over the document which said the farm and everything on it would revert to the bank in the case of John Bronson's death. *Why would he sign this?* Her eyes met the bankers. "Everything reverts to the bank? What about our house? Our furniture." *Our mother's things.*

The man shrugged. "It all belongs to the bank now, and has for two weeks. We've allowed you to stay so you had time to make other arrangements. I gather you haven't done that?" He looked disgusted that the two young women hadn't done anything to plan for their future.

Ellen shook her head. "We had no idea we should make other arrangements. May we have another week or two?" What they could do in that amount of time, she had no idea, but it would be something.

Mr. Baxter sighed. "I've already given you longer than I should have." He looked around at the rundown farm. "I'll tell you what. It's Tuesday. You can have until Friday to find somewhere to go, but then I'll have to take possession. I'll even let you keep your clothes. Nothing else, though." He climbed into the buggy to leave, obviously not caring how they felt about having three days to leave the only home they'd ever known.

"Three days isn't enough time!" Ellen cried in exasperation.

"It's all you have. Good day." He picked up the reigns and drove back toward Beckham.

Ellen looked at Malinda. "What do we do now?"

Malinda sighed. "We need to find jobs and a place to live.

We're old enough to work for wages." She kicked a rock toward the house. "I don't want to lose you!"

"You won't lose me. We'll find a way to stay close enough to see each other." Ellen took a deep breath to prepare mentally for the task at hand. "Well, there's no time like the present. Let's go change into our Sunday dresses and go to town."

"Where will we go? What's the best way to find a job?"

Ellen stepped back into the house. "We'll go to the mercantile, because there are often notices for employment there, and we can pick up the paper. Maybe there will be something there." She paused after climbing the stairs and looked at her sister. "I would like us to find something we can do together if possible. I don't want to lose the only family I have left."

Malinda hugged her sister. "I don't either. We'll find something together. I know we can."

Both quickly changed and washed their hands and faces before making the short walk into town. When they reached the mercantile, they went to the back of the store where the notices of people trying to sell things and people looking for employees were posted. The two sisters scanned through all the notes and found nothing.

They picked up a copy of the free paper and took it out to a bench in front of the store sitting on the boardwalk and watching the wagons and buggies drive by on the unpaved street in front of them. Ellen found the help wanted section of the paper, and since it was only two columns, read it silently, planning to read aloud if she saw something helpful. She reached the end of the column and sighed. "There are no jobs. Only one thing that may be helpful, but I don't think so." She made a face, not wanting to really consider the one thing.

"Well, something is better than nothing. Read it, and we'll

decide together what to do." Malinda looked at her sister eagerly, obviously hoping for something wonderful.

Ellen looked back down at the advertisement and read softly, "Mail Order Bride agency needs women who are looking for the adventure of their lives. Men out West need women to marry. Reply in person at 300 Rock Creek Road. See Mrs. Harriett Long."

Malinda looked at Ellen in surprise. "Mail Order Brides? Papa said we shouldn't marry until we were twenty one!"

Ellen nodded. "I know, but I don't think we have a choice. Let's go talk to Mrs. Long and see what she says. I don't see how she could possibly find us somewhere to go in just three days, but we'll see what happens. It's better than sitting here wondering what to do." Ellen really had no desire to be a mail order bride, because she was sure she couldn't find a man who would let her bring her younger sister along.

The sisters stood and walked to Rock Creek Road talking about the possibility. "We can't stay together if we become mail order brides!" Malinda protested.

"I thought of that, but maybe there will be two men in the same area looking for wives. If we live within an hour or two drive of each other, we'd at least be able to see each other on occasion."

"What do you think the chances of that are?"

Ellen laughed softly. "Probably next to nothing, but it's worth a try. Anything is worth a try, right?" Ellen's voice was desperately as she pled with her sister to at least try to talk to the woman from the ad.

They stopped short when they saw the house at the address. It was a huge brick house with large white columns in the front. "Wow. She's rich." Malinda wanted to bite her tongue after saying the words, but since she'd only said them to Ellen, they weren't terribly rude.

Ellen grinned at her sister. "Maybe Mrs. Long is the

cook." She started to walk up the sidewalk toward the door. She was nervous, but standing on the street staring at the house would only add to the nerves. She had always believed in doing what needed to be done quickly like taking a big dose of medicine.

Malinda followed her sister up to the door. "You know as well as I do Mrs. Long isn't the cook."

Ellen reached out and grabbed the door knocker bringing it down twice sharply. She put a hand over her stomach to still the butterflies and waited patiently. Within moments the door was pulled open. "May I help you?" The tall dark haired man at the door looked like he'd never smiled in his life.

Ellen swallowed hard. "I'm Ellen Bronson, and this is my sister, Malinda. We're here to see Mrs. Long."

The man gave one brief nod and opened the door wide. "If you'll just follow me, please?"

They followed him through the hallway. There was a staircase leading up to the second floor, but they walked around it toward the back of the house. He opened a door at the end of the hall and said, "Mrs. Long? There are two young ladies here to see you. They are both Miss Bronson."

The woman in the room got to her feet gracefully, walking toward them with a pronounced limp. "I'm Harriett Long. Come in and make yourselves comfortable." She had blond hair and warm green eyes. Ellen thought she looked like she was in her late twenties, but she wasn't certain.

"Thank you." Ellen headed toward the couch, leaving the chair behind the desk for Mrs. Long. It was where she'd been sitting, and she obviously had a great deal of work to do, because the desk was piled high.

Once Ellen and Malinda were seated on the sofa, and Mrs. Long was in front of the desk, the man asked, "Would you care for refreshments?"

"Please bring us some lemonade and some cookies if

there are some fresh. Thank you, Higgins." Mrs. Long faced the two young ladies and waited for one of them to say something as the man nodded regally and shut the door.

Ellen cleared her throat before beginning. "We're interested in your advertisement in the paper for mail order brides."

Mrs. Long nodded. "I'd surmised as much. How old are you?"

"I'm twenty, and my sister is nineteen."

"Old enough to marry, then. Good. I won't send out a young lady under the age of eighteen. Just one of my own little rules." Mrs. Long turned to her desk and set out a piece of paper and a pen. After dipping her pen in the pot of ink, she asked, "Why do you want to be mail order brides?"

Ellen and Malinda exchanged a look, and Ellen briefly wondered how much of the truth she should tell. She wouldn't lie to the woman, of course, but she didn't need to know the whole story did she? "Our father died two weeks ago, and we have no place to go. The bank is going to take possession of the farm, and everything on it in three days. We're only allowed to take our clothing. Nothing else."

Mrs. Long nodded, not seeming surprised by the story. "I understand." She studied the two girls for a moment. "Do you both want to become brides?"

Ellen nodded slowly. "We looked for jobs, but didn't see anything. We honestly have no idea what else to do." She reached over and gripped Malinda's hand. "We'd like to stay close together if possible, though."

"That may be difficult," Mrs. Long began. "I get letters from all over. It's not common to get two letters from the same area." She sat back in her chair as if she were thinking. "Wait! I got two letters yesterday from brothers in Colorado who are each looking for wives." She sorted through different papers on her desk and found the ones she was looking for. She handed both letters to Ellen.

Ellen skimmed the first and wrinkled her nose, passing it on to Malinda. The man was a banker, and she had no desire to marry someone who would treat anyone the way she and her sister had been treated that morning. She glanced at the second letter and immediately smiled. This was the letter for her. "My name is Wesley Harris. I'm twenty seven years old and the sheriff of the town of Gammonsville, Colorado. The town is at the foot of the Rocky Mountains. I moved out here with my brother in 1878 hoping to strike gold, but instead, I ended up being the sheriff and my brother opened the town bank. It's a quiet little town I think any woman would love living in. I'm looking for a woman who has never been married. I'd prefer someone who was between eighteen and twenty four, but that's flexible. Mainly I want a woman who isn't afraid of hard work who will take care of my home. I want children, so someone in good health is a necessity. I look forward to receiving a letter from you, so we can get to know one another and start a life together. Sincerely, Wesley Harris."

Ellen's smile lit up her face as her eyes met Mrs. Long's. "He's perfect for me. I want to marry the sheriff." She loved the idea of marrying a man who put his life on the line every day to help others. Wesley Harris was definitely the man for her.

Malinda had finished her letter around the same time and nodded. "I love the idea of marrying the banker."

Ellen made a face. "You would." Her sister would make a good wife for a rich man. Ellen was positive the banker was made for her.

Malinda sighed. "I don't ever want to be poor again. We're losing the only home we've ever had. I can't imagine how anyone would choose not to marry a man with money."

Mrs. Long smiled at the sisters. "So do you want to respond to their letters?" Her voice and tone told Ellen that even though this was obviously a business for her, she cared about the women she sent West.

Ellen nodded. "How long does the whole process take? We have three days to get out of our house. Is there any way we can leave in that amount of time?"

Mrs. Long stared at them both for a moment before responding. "Normal process time is around two months depending on how quickly the men respond and how many letters are exchanged before you go. Colorado letters take around three weeks, so we're looking at a minimum of six weeks."

Ellen stood up. "I think we're wasting your time. Thanks for speaking with us." She gave a longing look to the letter she'd set down on the table in front of the sofa. She'd liked the man who'd written the letter and would have loved to have been able to meet him and marry him. They couldn't wait six weeks, though. It just wasn't possible. They'd have to find something else, and every minute they spent talking to Mrs. Long was a wasted minute.

Malinda sat looking between Ellen and Mrs. Long as if she were trying to decide whether to go with Ellen or try to find some way to marry the man who'd written the letter in her hand.

Mrs. Long seemed to think about the situation for a moment as she watched the two girls. "I have a proposition for you. This house is much too big for me. I have plenty of space for the two of you to stay with me. I've also got so much work to do with my business that I'm falling behind. I've considered hiring someone to help me, but after the month it would take to catch up, there would only be an hour or so per day of work, and no one is looking for a job for one day per week. So, if you will, stay with me and in exchange for room and board, help me catch up my work."

Ellen bit her lip as she considered. She knew Mrs. Long was basically offering them charity, but at that point, she didn't see any other choices. Maybe they could find other ways to help out as well. She nodded slowly. "We'd be happy to do that. I think we need to do more than just help with your business, though. Is there anything else we could do to earn our keep?"

"Sit down, and we'll talk about it. If I run out of work for you to do, we'll come up with something."

Ellen resumed her seat on the couch and looked down at the letter. "He does sound perfect for me."

Mrs. Long, who had risen to her feet when Ellen did, sank slowly into her chair obviously favoring one leg. "Let's write some letters then, shall we?" She handed them each a piece of paper and a pen, putting a small pot of ink between them. "I'd like you to include age, occupation if there is one, a brief description of yourself, and any hobbies you may have."

Both of the sisters put pen to paper and began writing. Ellen thought for a moment after writing the salutation, trying to decide exactly what she wanted to tell him. "Dear Wesley, I was thrilled to receive your letter. I'm twenty years old and live on the outskirts of Beckham, Massachusetts where I've lived my entire life. I was raised on a small dairy farm, and enjoy being around animals. I like the idea of living in a small town near the Rocky Mountains. I've only ever seen paintings of mountains and love the idea of seeing one in person. I have kept house for my father since my mother died when I was twelve, so I'm more than capable of cooking and cleaning for you. I love the idea of having a houseful of children. I'm in good health. My sister is answering the letter your brother sent. We love the idea of being mail order brides, but living close together. I enjoy reading and taking long walks. I hope to hear from you soon. Yours, Ellen."

Ellen set the pen down and handed the letter to Mrs. Long. "Is that what you're looking for?"

Mrs. Long quickly read through the letter and then nodded. "It's perfect."

Ellen watched as her sister wrote quickly trying to finish her own letter. Finally, Malinda looked up and handed it to Mrs. Long as well. "How's that?"

"Good." Mrs. Long folded both letters and set them aside. "We'll get them mailed out first thing in the morning." She looked up as Higgins came into the room with the lemonade and cookies she'd requested. He set the tray in front of her and she poured them each a glass, and set the plate with the cookies on it between them. "Thank you, Higgins."

Ellen picked up the glass of lemonade and took a sip of the tart liquid. She and Malinda had cut back to cooking one meal per day in hopes they could make the food last, so she was thankful for the cookies. She reached out and took one and smiled. "These are good!" She counted the cookies on the plate and divided mentally by three wondering how many she could eat without looking like a glutton.

Mrs. Long smiled as Higgins shut the door behind him. "My cook is wonderful." She took a cookie for herself as the girls settled back onto the couch to enjoy the small snack. "Do you girls have what you need to stay at the farm for the rest of the week, or do you just want to move in here tomorrow?" She gestured to the pile of letters on her desk. "I could use the help."

Ellen looked at Malinda. If they went home, they wouldn't be able to eat. It made more sense to move immediately. "What do you think, Malinda?"

Malinda tilted her head to the side in a way that told Ellen she was thinking about it. "I think we should go ahead and move right away. I don't want to be there when they come to take all of our things away."

Ellen hadn't thought about how hard that would be. Of course, since she'd been giving most of the food to Malinda, she was thinking more with her stomach than her emotions. She squeezed Malinda's hand. "Why don't we come back in the morning then? Would that be okay?"

Mrs. Long nodded. "We'll be thrilled to have you."

Once they'd polished off the cookies and lemonade, Ellen stood. "We'll pack our things this evening and be back around ten tomorrow morning. Would that be okay?" She considered for a moment all the work Mrs. Long said she had for them. "Is that early enough?"

Mrs. Long stood and walked them toward the door. "That would be wonderful. I'll enjoy having company for a while."

Ellen smiled at the older woman. "Thank you so much for your hospitality. We truly appreciate the help you're giving us." She shook Mrs. Long's hand. "We'll work hard. I promise."

"I know you will. I'll see you in the morning." Closing the door behind them, she called Higgins. "We're going to be having some guests for a while."

*****

Ellen baked the last of the corn bread that evening and as they ate it, they talked about the letters. "I love the idea of marrying a banker!" Malinda gushed. "Just imagine not having to worry about money. And he said he has a cook and someone who cleans! I'd have all the time I wanted to read books and just keep to myself. He's going to be perfect for me!" Malinda's eyes danced with excitement at the prospect of marrying her banker.

Ellen sighed. "Don't you think it's more important that he be a good person than he make a lot of money? The sheriff sounds like the kind of man I'm looking for. He wouldn't put his life on the line every day if he didn't think helping others was important." Her sister had never been materialistic, but she hated all of her time being taken up by chores. It had been better before their father died, because then they were only doing the housework, and not all of the farm work as well.

"Maybe. I'm glad you're the one marrying him, though. I'm tired of housework. You can have it all!" Malinda waved her arm as if to encompass the entire house full of work she was gifting to her sister.

"I'd gladly do housework every day of my life if it meant I didn't have to marry a man who would kick grieving people out of the only home they've ever known. How could you even think of marrying a banker after what happened this morning?" Ellen was stunned at her sister's attitude. Sure, housework wasn't the most fun thing to do in the world, but it was better than sitting idle while the man you were married to was out being cruel to others.

"How could you even think of not marrying the richest man you can find after what happened this morning?" Malinda shook her head in confusion.

Ellen shook her head at her younger sister. "I think we'll have to agree to disagree on this one." She stood up. "Let's get these dishes done so we can go pack our things."

Before they went to bed that evening, everything the sisters owned was in a huge trunk. It was good they were going to the same place, because there was only one. In the back of her mind, Ellen felt bad for taking the trunk after being told they could only take their clothing, but she knew they simply didn't have a choice unless they wanted to walk down the streets of Beckham with their drawers in their arms. She wasn't willing to make that kind of spectacle of herself, though.

When Ellen prayed that night, she thanked God for bringing Harriett Long into their lives. She was truly their guardian angel. She went to sleep with a smile on her lips as she thought about the good man she'd marry. Any man who cared enough for others to do a job where he must risk his life on a daily basis was one she had to admire.

ALSO BY KIRSTEN OSBOURNE

Sign up for instant notification of all of Kirsten's New Releases Text
'BOB' to 42828

And

For a complete list of Kirsten's works head to her website
wwww.kirstenandmorganna.com

ABOUT THE AUTHOR

www.kirstenandmorganna.com

Printed in the USA
CPSIA information can be obtained
at www.ICGtesting.com
LVHW012138310824
789834LV00005B/257